Sojourners Through Time

John Frederick Zurn

Published by Everlasting Light, Yorkville, IL, 2023.

Sojourners Through Time
by John Frederick Zurn

.

.

.

.

Everlasting Light Publishing
Yorkville, IL USA

.

.

Cover page photo by Greg Rakozy courtesy of Unsplash.Com
https://unsplash.com/photos/oMpAz-DN-9I

Table of Contents

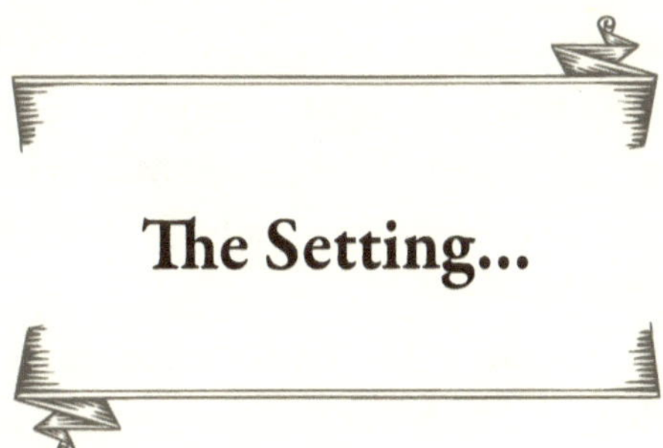

The Setting...

A time of crisis looms over the ancient world of Durgana. Emperor Sutin and his warriors rule with cruelty, greed, and ambition. Most villagers live in poverty and despair while they attempt to simply survive.

Spared from the emperor's brutality, a fifteen year old girl named Sita and her family live on a farm where they remain poor, but self-sufficient. Ignorant of the condition of the world, Sita and her family live in a small friendly village. Despite Sita's struggle with relationships because of her inability to hear, she spends her time helping the family and reading adventure books.

Yet, Sita's humility and self-sacrifice soon attracts the attention of a Great Mystic name Dharmaji. After witnessing her good character, Dharmaji appears to her in the form of a vision of light. Having decided that Sita might prove to be a worthy addition to the Great One's group, Dharmaji asks her to participate in three difficult tasks that are essential to her possible entry into the group. He proves his good intentions and power by curing Sita of her deafness.

Ironically, Sita has serious problems with all three scenarios she is required to solve. These tasks include living with the Crimson Plaque, creating stories that come to life, and attempting to rescue a village from a witch. Even though she doesn't do particularly well with her three challenges, Dharmaji accepts her into the group because he recognizes her potential.

As the mission to save Durgana begins in earnest, Sita meets other beings who will help renew the light. Atmun the shapeshifter, Deudal the birdman from the Treeganaut race, and Minerva, the enchantress. Sita feels inferior to all of them, but gradually she must discover ways to become useful to the team.

Nonetheless, it appears highly unlikely that this unique group can defeat Emperor Sutin and his armies. Yet they still risk their lives in their quest to save Durgana. Although their numbers are few, when Minerva and Dharmaji reveal their true identities, hope returns to the group. Sita, especially has faith because of all her difficult experiences prior to the actual mission. They've taught her courage and promoted her maturity.

As the story begins, Sita has no inclination about the danger her family may encounter. When Dharmaji first contacts her in the bright white light, her life changes forever. Only Dharmaji "the Great One," knows the path Sita must walk in order to save Durgana and her family from centuries of increasing darkness....

Crisis In Durgana

This is the story of Durgana, an ancient civilization that existed at a time when fear and darkness still controlled the race of mortals. It was an age of selfishness and suffering, when petty dictators wielded their weapons of conquest in order to realize their ruthless ambitions for power. The days of the heroes were now long gone; and the beings of this hapless planet seemed lost in the misery of poverty, and all the suffering that these social ills create. Their burdens overwhelmed them, and their chances for prosperity remained elusive.

These impoverished mortals knew only tedious work in the worn out fields or exhausting labor in the dark and dangerous mines. For many, the certainty of their inevitable deaths provided one of the few hopes they dared to contemplate. In a perilous land cursed with perpetual moral darkness and utter despair, the time of deliverance appeared to be rapidly slipping away.

Surprisingly, this downward slide toward the abyss went somewhat unchallenged by the vast population of mortal beings who toiled in this fallen world. Despite their lot, these citizens knew of almost nothing else, so they accepted their plight as inevitable.

Nevertheless, they did allow themselves one wavering belief that their wicked rulers invented and then spread. These tyrants trusted the world of war and political intrigue. Portraying their dangerous plans as harbingers of peace and worthy of support, these leaders engaged in persuasion and intimidation to both deceive the people and satisfy their desire for conquest.

Then, of course, weapons appeared that promised deterrence and protection. Yet, always in the end, when negotiations inevitably failed; wars began, and the Durgana world soon erupted in violence. With each passing century, the practice of combat became ever more deadly, and millions perished in the relentless conflicts. Like an unstoppable plague, this obsession with conquest eventually annihilated entire populations and ground the natural world to dust. Now, after centuries of war and the destruction of the natural world, the planet had succumbed to the foul smelling air, the poisonous rivers, and the deforestation of ancient forests.

But the wars alone hadn't ravaged the natural world. Centuries of unregulated commerce and unrestrained science could also be blamed for the dire condition of Durgana. The digging of mines and drilling for oil also created environmental disasters. Every part of the natural world, no matter how remote or pristine, came to be exploited. This destruction continued relentlessly simply to fill the bank accounts of the acquisitive leaders whose insatiable greed seemed unquenchable. Government scientists, for their part, constantly tortured the world's most innocent creatures in order to test their more deadly weapons.

Sita Encounters a Luminous Being

However, there existed an ancient prophecy. Thousands of years earlier, a great sage from the East had predicted this era of darkness and the widespread destruction and despair that would accompany it. This holy man predicted he would return and turn back the tidal wave of war and despair. Then the poor would know prosperity and the natural world would be renewed. In this new age of light and love, the behavior of the rich would recognize the truth of existence, while the impoverished multitudes would be liberated at last.

Understandably, after thousands of years, this prophecy had become so tangled up with fiction and folklore it had been ultimately relegated to the story teller's campfire. In time, even these sources lost much of their credibility, and so the words and wisdom of the "Great Ones" slowly began to slip away. Without the support of even an oral tradition, the legend faced the danger of disappearing forever.

However, one fifteen year old girl named Sita still believed despite her abject poverty. She was one of the billions of innocent children engulfed by hardship who seemed destined to live a short, miserable life; yet she remained oblivious to her plight.

Fortunately, like most children, she didn't truly understand the hopelessness of her circumstances. In her innocence and charity, she could be cheerful, enthusiastic, and willing to help others. Although Sita appeared short in stature and slender in build, she could work for hours in the hot sun with her parents. Sita could even be described as courageous because she accepted and managed her deafness even though it made it difficult for her to communicate with other children.

Instead of feeling sorry for herself, Sita spent her days helping to raise her young twin brothers, Jeremy and Adam. She remained indispensable to her family because of her energetic nature and her emotional maturity. Her hard working attitude offered relief, especially for her parents, because she completed her chores without supervision and helped Jeremy and Adam with their chores and school work.

Because she could barely hear since birth, Sita had long ago learned the value of books. Safe within their pages, she hid from a silent world that she couldn't understand. The young fifteen year old child eventually borrowed and read so many books that she could imagine an entire universe within her mind. This ability freed her from the indifferent world around her and instilled a personal sense of belonging. Since she could only hear words when they were spoken very close to her, other children often ignored her. Even worse, they sometimes gossiped about her even when she stood near them. Since Sita could sometimes read lips, she could occasionally understand their conversations, but chose to ignore their cruelty. Instead, she sought out the imaginative companions she encountered in stories. Over time, she lived more and more within her own world of noble ideas and loving relationships, and that appeared to be enough for her. Ironically, it was actually through this same fascination with books that Sita discovered the ancient sage known as Thought Healer.

Surprisingly, Sita's understanding of this Great Being didn't come directly from any one book or even from someone else in the village. Instead, the Thought Healer appeared as a kind of vision in which her thoughts and feelings dissolved and in their place a brilliant light emerged. As Sita watched this extraordinary light with both stillness and awareness, she observed a luminous being slowly approaching. She courageously held her inner gaze on the miraculous image and then he spoke, "Do not be frightened, my child. You are safe with me. I am very pleased that you have found me in my secret haven behind the Durgana world."

Sita initially felt startled when the being began to speak, but his soft voice and calming words convinced her that he couldn't be some demon or malevolent ghost. "Why have you come here to see me?" she asked as her self-confidence slowly returned. "Are you a warrior who has come to conquer the Durgana realm?"

"No child, I am not," the being replied simply.

"Then who are you, if you don't mind me asking?" Sita continued, becoming bolder.

"I am Dharmaji, the Cosmic Being, and I'm here to restore Durgana," the great being asserted.

"I thought you only existed as an intriguing story," Sita replied in bewilderment.

"To most, I am a story or less," Dharmaji answered frowning. "Yet, you have discovered me here in my place of seclusion. Now, I am here to help you, but I also need your help as well."

"I'm just a girl," Sita replied apprehensively. "I'm not old enough or smart enough to help you. Not only that, I'm almost totally deaf. I'm no use to anyone except my family. I don't even know how I'm able to hear you now."

Dharmaji smiled and the brilliant light surrounding him soon transformed into a rose color with light indigo surrounding it. This magnificent radiance appeared to be saturated with so much love that it nearly overwhelmed Sita's capacity to bear it. When this beautiful light became absorbed back into the mystic's being again, he said, "Sita, you have been of great assistance to others. Because of your facility and humility, you haven't realized all the good you've been doing for others. The very fact that you found my secret location provides proof enough for me that you have the ability to help me."

Sita still felt confused and a little unsettled by Dharmaji's remarks about her life, yet the wondrous vision had also given her courage. "I still don't understand!" she blurted out. "Are you here to help my family and the village?"

Dharmaji remained impressed with Sita's attitude. Even though she seemed to be barely more than a child, she still considered the needs of others above her own. He smiled again at her and answered, "Sita, since you remain the only one who has been able to reach me; you must share my burden. With your help, we must rescue your world from those who are unknowingly destroying it."

Sita, still remained unaware of the perils of the outside world, and she did not comprehend what Dharmaji had been describing. "What's wrong with the world? Isn't it mostly good? Other children sometimes tease me, but my family loves me."

"I know," he replied. "But your views of the world don't extend beyond the village, and your books are mostly stories of adventure. Their ideas have no sustainable purpose or wisdom. You know little about hatred, ambition, and war. Until now, you've been protected. Nevertheless, we've chosen each other for this difficult and dangerous task. So, we must see it through to the end together."

Sita began to feel an uneasy sense of obligation envelop her now. It felt like a more important duty than taking care of her brothers or working in the fields with her parents. Suddenly, she felt she had been chosen, not because she appeared to be the same as everyone else, but because she happened to be different from them. It felt like a haze had now been lifted from her mind, and she could see clearly for the first time. "Yes, I'll go with you," Sita replied with more self-confidence. "What do you need me to do?"

Dharmaji spoke even more mysteriously now, as he told Sita about his intended plan. "You must come back to this same meeting place tomorrow at dawn, and keep our meeting secret. At that time, I'll show you many things about our world that you haven't yet discovered. It will be difficult for you. After that we'll discuss the mission. When you leave here today, I'll permanently restore your hearing; however, you must pretend that your hearing is the same as before. If your family and the villagers discern the truth, it will bring out emotions in them that you will be compelled to bear."

Sita felt so preoccupied by Dharmaji's appearance and mysterious words that she had forgotten entirely about her deafness. But, when she finally realized what had happened, her joy and gratitude overwhelmed her, and she began to weep, "Thank you," she wept softly. "I won't let you down, I promise." Then she added hastily, "But I'm still confused. How will I find you? I only found you this time by chance."

"Don't worry," Dharmaji responded. "I'll find you if you come by this stream again tomorrow at dawn. Now I must go. Remember what I told you."

"Wait!" exclaimed Sita. "Please stay a little longer."

Before Sita could finish her question, Dharmaji had already merged into the dazzling light and then disappeared.

The very next moment, Sita could hear the world around her clearly for the first time. A symphony of sounds astounded her, as if she had entered a magical realm. Every sound she could perceive now existed as more than a vibration; it felt almost like a mystical experience. Singing birds in the willows and the sounds of the gurgling stream behind her house became intensely real, as if they possessed a secret fragrance and cool intensity. As she scampered through the village, she could hear her family and neighbors chattering away, and her entire world seemed new and fresh like the tangible thrill of a sunrise.

When Sita finally returned home, she could barely conceal her excitement and enthusiasm, and before long, she forgot about Dharmaji's injunction. Her mother first noticed the change in her daughter, as she watched Sita skipping across the backyard patio. "Sita, why do you seem so cheerful?" she asked.

Sita slowed herself down, finally recalling her promise to Dharmaji, and resumed her natural attitude of meekness and silence. She tried her best to remember how she had acted before Dharmaji had miraculously healed and she replied softly, "It's such a beautiful day, and I just feel happy."

That answer would have been satisfactory if Sita hadn't later made one blatant, yet understandable mistake. While she sat by the fireplace cooking supper, her father called from the back patio asking, "Can somebody help me out here?"

Sita immediately turned away from the fireplace and yelled back, "I'll be right there, father

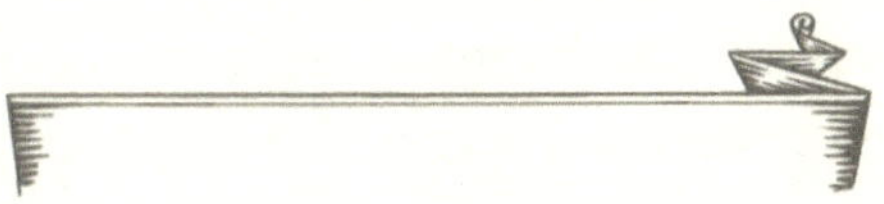

Sita Learns about Suffering and Death

Sita's mother felt stunned by her daughter's sudden ability to hear. She whirled around, stepped over to her, and tapped her daughter deliberately on the shoulder, exclaiming, "Sita how could you hear what your father said? How could you understand him?"

Sita immediately realized her mistake. In the excitement of experiencing her miraculous cure, she had unintentionally revealed her secret; the most important instruction that Dharmaji had given to her only hours before. Now, if she didn't explain herself satisfactorily, she might lose the chance to accompany him on his mysterious quest. She thought hard for a moment and then a quickly formulated plan arose in her mind. She pulled her notebook from her pocket and wrote down one single word – "What?"

Her mother slowly returned to a calmer state of mind, then gazed at Sita again and asked her about her sudden ability to respond to her father's voice. Sita pretended to be confused and responded, "You know I always talk to myself. Did father say something?"

Sita's response satisfied her mother; but Sita also felt deeply saddened by her mother's spontaneous expression of joy that now seemed entirely unfounded. She gently touched her daughter's chin, and they all went back to their chores.

Sita began to weep silently, and she quickly turned away the moment her mother left her side. She had so wanted to express her joy and reassure her devoted family about her miraculous experience with Dharmaji. But, somehow she knew that for whatever reasons, he felt it must be important for her to follow his instructions. So, in order to keep her secret, Sita pretended she couldn't hear at all. As she swept the small four room cottage, however, her sense of curiosity and adventure awakened once more.

The next day, long before dawn, Sita quietly hurried through her chores. She gathered firewood and filled the clay water jugs at the stream. Then she fed and milked Gana, the family cow. Finally, when she had finished, she took one last glance at her home, and then sprinted out to the meadow near the hemlock forest. When she found the rustic stream where she had first met Dharmaji, she sat down, calmed herself, and slowed her breathing.

She sat quietly for a while, until she could feel her racing thoughts subside, and then she softly closed her eyes. She gazed within at her thoughts and inner images for several minutes but nothing happened. She maintained her attitude of quiet persistence for several more minutes but failed to see Dharmaji. Disappointed and frustrated, Sita eventually gave up; however, she also remembered the mystic's secretive promise that he would find her, so she resigned herself to scanning for him in the outer landscape around her. She decided to remain by the stream in silence and patiently wait for his arrival.

Before long, Sita observed Dharmaji standing upstream near the woods. Although barely visible, his long, jet black hair, orange tunic, and dark piercing eyes were easily discernable even at a distance. She immediately jumped up and ran toward him; but as she approached, he seemed to move farther away. After a few minutes, Sita realized the Great Being appeared to be leading her into the forest itself.

By the time Sita caught up with Dharmaji, she felt exhausted, bewildered, and wanted an explanation. The Mystic Being, however, quickly interrupted and gently scolded her. "You must learn to follow instructions, child. I can't always explain things to you; you must learn to trust me."

"But my mother seemed so happy and then so disappointed," Sita complained.

"Yes, I know," Dharmaji replied. "But I have my reasons. I can't hurry because you're hurrying. Sometimes we must do many things at once."

"I don't understand," Sita complained.

The Dharmaji tried again to explain himself. "Before taking a trip, one must load the wagon and hitch up the oxen, is it not so?"

"Yes," Sita answered, finally understanding. "We have to pack up everything carefully or the trip may not go well."

"That's right," The Great Being replied assuredly. "Patience and faith are important virtues to possess. So, with that in mind, I have a very important task for you to accomplish. It will also be an important lesson for you to learn as you prepare for our journey."

"What is it?" Sita asked more enthusiastically now.

Dharmaji pointed to an outcropping of lichen covered boulders and said, "I want you to walk past those boulders and then tell me what you find."

At first, Sita remained silent because she felt extremely disappointed with the Dharmaji's request, thinking he could be sending her on some simple nature hike or childish scavenger hunt. She stared at him coolly and said, "I don't have much time, my parents will be waiting for me."

"Beyond those boulders, there's something you must see," Dharmaji replied simply, as he abruptly turned to leave her.

The Great One's obscure remark reassured Sita and reignited her curiosity. She dashed up to the huge rocks, crossed over, and then hiked into a gully below. She searched everywhere anticipating that she would make some wonderful discovery or solve some important mystery. But, after a while, she began to sense that something seemed very wrong.

In her desire to discover Dharmaji's secret, she somehow lost her way. The boulders she recently crossed disappeared and when she hustled back up the ridge, both Dharmaji and the stream vanished as well. A feeling of uncertainty and dread began to grow in Sita's mind until she finally started to panic. Wandering in circles, she realized that she had never been so lost and frightened in her life.

At last, in utter desperation, Sita climbed a gigantic willow tree; and there, a few miles away, she could barely perceive the outline of a secluded settlement. At first, it seemed like a tempting mirage, but when the image remained stable, Sita decided to investigate. From her vantage point, she carefully noted various landmarks that she could employ as trail markers such as unusual rock formations and lopsided pine trees. Then, when she felt ready, she climbed back down the tree and hurried through the forest, hoping she wouldn't be caught alone in the unfamiliar woods at night.

By the time Sita reached the surprisingly well fortified town, twilight began to descend; she felt relieved to have finally escaped the forest. However, this feeling of security soon abandoned her when she passed through the town's open gate. As she looked around, she thought it peculiar that a village surrounded by such formidable walls should have an unsecured entrance. Yet, when she passed through the unguarded entrance and walked to the cobblestone street, Sita understood why the gate remained open.

Everyone in the town appeared to be dead! In the street, people of all ages were lying in rigid grotesque positions with strange sores oozing from their bodies and faces. In front of every house and shop, corpses appeared sprawled out on the sidewalk, as if they had fallen dead where they stood. The dead could be seen stacked up like wood at both the church and livery stable. The only prominent signs on the buildings seemed to be red crosses on doors and windows. The faces of the deceased appeared to be panic stricken and tormented. But, worst of all, a stench filled the air. The odor of rotting flesh contaminated the air, encouraging the squabbling turkey vultures that sounded wildly excited by the foul decay.

Sita felt terrified and confused. She couldn't be entirely certain what had happened to these poor dead beings, but she knew she they were beyond her help now. As she walked to the far edge of the town, the awful stench of death became even more poignant. Sita hesitantly decided to find out why. Covering her nose with her sleeve, she walked toward the source of the awful odor and discovered over a dozen wagons loaded with the diseased remains of children and adults. As she forced herself to move past them, she soon encountered a gigantic pit with bodies littered at the bottom or snagged against the jagged dirt walls. She turned away in horror, and not knowing what to do, she returned to the disease infested village.

As twilight gave way to the darkness, Sita stared at the dead bodies trying to comprehend what had occurred. She found a torch outside a livery stable, and then lit it. Sita couldn't decide whether it would be more dangerous to remain in the village or return to the uncertainties of the forest at night. Meanwhile, as she continued brooding over her dilemma, Sita heard the unmistakable sound of a child calling out to her. She immediately followed the voice until suddenly a boy appeared from behind a building. When he drew closer, Sita stood still, not knowing what to do. The boy seemed puzzled as well and waited for her to make the first move.

Before long, however, Sita's compassionate nature asserted itself, and she approached the boy and embraced him. His clothes smelled like filthy rags, and scars appeared all over his neck and arms. Despite the boy's appearance, Sita overlooked his possible illness. She felt so relieved to find another living soul that she held him for a long time. The young boy soon began weeping and slowly let his emotions spill out. After a few moments, Sita asked him, "What's your name?"

"My name is Dukka," the boy answered. "I'm the only one left."

"My name is Sita. What happened here?"

The boy spoke haltingly as he told Sita about the dreadful events he had witnessed. "This spring, a group of soldiers from the city of

Galaway arrived in our village, and spent all week hunting in the nearby forests. On the fourth day of their visit, the village physician realized that the soldiers had all contracted a terrible sickness called the Crimson Plague. When the doctor informed the mayor, the mayor panicked. Both he and the physician fled the village in the middle of the night. By the time the villagers discovered the truth, many of them had also become infected; and it wasn't long before the soldiers and all the villagers either fled or died."

"What about you?" Sita asked slowly, trying to comprehend the horror of the plague. "Why aren't you sick?"

Dukka remained silent for a very long time but finally replied, "I did become sick, terribly sick. But I didn't die like the others, and the plague left me after a few days. In the entire village, I'm the only survivor. Now you must go."

Sita felt very confused and somewhat frightened by Dukka's account of the Crimson Plague, but she knew she would never forgive herself if she left the boy behind. She did, however, need to convince him to trust her. "I can't go into the forest alone again," she asserted diplomatically, "and you can't stay here with all this terrible disease and death. So, I'm not staying here and neither are you. Now please lead us through the forest."

At first, Dukka refused, fearing for Sita's safety, but then he realized that Sita might actually abandon him if he remained in the village, so he ultimately agreed to accompany her. He then took charge and began guiding Sita through the dense pine forest and treacherous thickets. As they pressed on, Dukka finally revealed to Sita where they needed to go. "We must travel to Galaway," he asserted confidentially. "It's a magnificent city with many rich nobles and clever healers. We must find out more about the Crimson Plague that wiped out my village and nearly killed me."

"Why?" Sita asked innocently. "You're all right now, and no one else needs saving."

"Except you," Dukka replied.

Then Sita finally understood the terrible risk she had taken by entering the village. In her own little town, people got hurt or sick and even died, but they never died in large numbers or in such a horrible way. For the first time in her life, Sita understood the concept of death as a cataclysmic event. She shook with fear when she realized that she could actually contract this terrifying disease.

Despite her trepidation, Sita managed to consider Dukka's remarkable recovery more clearly, and began to understand he might be a very unusual child.

Even though both his parents succumbed to the Crimson Plaque, and he had barely escaped it himself, Dukka still seemed able to express compassion and concern for her even though he barely knew her. As Sita's panic of contracting the disease gradually subsided, she hiked behind her young friend until dawn. Then, after a brief respite, they made their way toward Galaway.

By the time they reached the small villages surrounding the city, the evidence of the plague appeared everywhere. Businesses and cottages boarded up and locked from the outside, left only the very ill and the dead visible on the streets. Foul smelling corpses were piled up behind the hotel and in front of the churches, and vermin freely scurried around unchallenged. It sickened Sita to witness such suffering and stench, but she followed Dukka anyway. As she followed close behind him, he cautiously eluded the grasp of the dying who constantly pleaded for help. He understood that these poor souls were dead already, and so he and Sita hurried on ignoring their awful cries. At last, a number of square two story structures appeared directly ahead of them, and they realized they had reached their destination. The metropolis of Galaway now stood directly in front of them.

When they had reached the outskirts of the city, Sita and Dukka immediately were accosted by an exceedingly old soldier who stood guard at the massive gate. Although the guard appeared fearless at first, when he spoke his tone revealed a feeling of weariness and dread. "Who are you and what do you want?" the guard bellowed attempting to sound threatening.

"I am Dukka and this is my friend, Sita," the boy responded cautiously. "We must speak with your physicians about the plague. We seek a cure."

The melancholy guard suddenly started to laugh and blurted out, "Cure? What cure? Everyone is sick! If a cure existed, don't you think we would have already given it to the sick and dying?"

"Could we just speak with a doctor?" Dukka continued pressing his point.

"Look!" the guard answered angrily, losing his patience. "Nobody can enter or leave the city, and that includes you two presumptuous children!"

Dukka and Sita initially seemed very disappointed, but when they turned away from the gate, the guard did something completely unexpected. He groaned piteously and fell down dead. Astonished, they both stared down at the pale, old man, and immediately Sita chose to interpret his death as a warning. She once again felt overwhelmed by the plague's cruelty and couldn't comprehend how a person could be standing one moment and then be dead on the ground a moment later. Confusion and fear swept through her mind again, and she felt overcome with distress.

But Dukka recovered his composure more quickly having grown accustomed to the horror of the plague in his own village. Unlike Sita, he realized the guard's death provided them an opportunity to pass through the gate and into the city of Galaway. He grabbed her by the hand, and hurriedly jogged down the cobblestone streets. Then they passed under the dilapidated structures which once served as shops and residences.

As in Dukka's village, the shadow of death appeared, dark and deep. Every doorway and street corner was strewn with dead bodies, and crows feasting on both human and animal remains. The scene closely resembled the aftermath of a battlefield or natural disaster with no one left alive to bury the dead.

However, as they searched diligently for any physician's office, Dukka and Sita began to discern that some citizens actually turned out to be very much alive. It appeared that they had either locked themselves in the upper rooms of various residences, in order to keep others out, or they had been forcibly locked in and couldn't escape. Some unfortunate souls even remained behind boxes and barrels in the cellars of these plague-ridden dwellings.

As they hurried along with both uncertainty and alarm, Sita and Dukka finally located a physician's shingle hanging above a half opened door. They both immediately stepped inside and startled a man behind the counter who had been making some kind of foul smelling potion. "Are you a doctor?" Dukka asked.

"Yes I am," the man asserted.

He looked shabbily dressed, and it appeared he hadn't bathed for at least a week. There also seemed to be a sense of desperation in his pale face that he tried to conceal, but it seemed unmistakable. "I'm the doctor," he repeated. "How can I help you?"

Sita sensed that the man's attempt to look relaxed could be merely a ruse, so she decided to challenge him. "Sir," she challenged. "How are you treating this plaque that has stricken the citizens of Galaway?"

The man muttered some incoherent words repeatedly and then, unexpectedly, sat down and began to weep. "I know this isn't my office and I'm trespassing," he sobbed miserably. "But the real physicians have all died or run off, and my wife has become very ill. All our children have been lost, and only my wife remains. I'm trying to save her life. Please don't have me arrested."

Sita felt deeply moved by the man's distress and devotion, as she watched the tears trickle down his grief stricken face. However, she also began to believe that their own search for a cure might be beyond their grasp. After considering the situation carefully, Sita concluded that her only hope for survival depended on her staying healthy. However, this strategy didn't seem very realistic especially considering the circumstances.

Even still, after seeing the man's agony, Sita decided to comfort him and take on the burden of caring for his wife. "What's your name?" Sita asked sweetly. "And who's your wife?"

"My name is Thomas, miss," he answered. "And my wife is Sophia."

"All right" Sita answered. "Now, take me to your home," Sita directed.

Thomas walked out of the physician's office and into the street, while Dukka and Sita followed behind. As they all turned the corner, they suddenly became aware of hysterical townspeople banging on doors and windows from inside various buildings. This resembled the startling scene of locked shops and houses that they had witnessed briefly when they first arrived in Galaway. "Who's locked up in all these buildings?" Sita called out.

Thomas stopped only long enough to explain. "If someone gets sick in any building, they lock everyone inside."

Sita felt dumfounded. "Are you saying that if anyone in a building is infected, everyone else must be locked up with them?"

"Yes," Thomas responded more impatiently. "It helps to control the spread of the contagion."

"But it doesn't," Dukka replied simply. "Almost everyone dies no matter what precautions are taken." Locking people up in their houses really hasn't helped.

Dukka's remarks moved Sita deeply, and she felt the need to respond to the anguished cries of the imprisoned citizens who suffered all around her. She decided to find a way to unbolt all the structures regardless of who might be in them. So when they reached Thomas's house, Sita agreed to help Sophia; however, she also directed Thomas and Dukka to open all the condemned buildings and free the captives who remained locked inside. They both reluctantly agreed, but Thomas seemed very frightened and uneasy as he said goodbye to his wife.

As soon as they were gone, Sita went to Sophia's bedside and tried to comfort her with cold compresses, sips of water, and compassionate words. In only a matter of hours, however, with Thomas and Dukka still somewhere in the city; Sophia's health quickly deteriorated and death appeared to be fast approaching, so Sita made one last attempt to reassure her. "Sophia, soon you'll be free from your pain and suffering. Then this illness will no longer have any power over you. Your troubles will be over."

Sophia smiled weakly, then took her last few agonizing breaths, and said, "But now your troubles have just begun."

Sophia's cryptic remarks surprised and puzzled Sita, and she stared at Sophia's lifeless body in bewildered silence. However, before long, she understood the meaning of Sophia's' prophetic words. As she turned to leave the room, she noticed a stinging sensation originating on her forehead and felt a grotesquely shaped nodule throbbing against her irritated neck. Sita stood completely still, shocked and disorientated, and then fled from the house in terror.

Sita then rushed into the street in despair nearly stumbling over the dead and dying who existed everywhere. In a state of utter panic, she shrieked out Dukka's name and frantically searched the city for both Thomas and her friend. Almost immediately, however, she became light headed and nauseated, and the buildings around her seemed to spin. Finally, she collapsed on the street, delirious from fever that now infected her mind and body.

Fortunately, Dukka and Thomas heard Sita's anguished cries for help and rushed to her side. They tried to comfort her, but she now felt too feeble to appear grateful. Instead, her voice sounded strained and her strength quickly abandoning her.

Thomas, moved by Sita's plight, also remained very concerned about his wife's well-being, and he couldn't resist asking Sita about her. "Sita," he asked hesitantly, "How is my Sophia?"

In her suffering and alarm, Sita had completely forgotten about Sophia. She now felt so ill; she became much more concerned for her own survival. Finally, she whispered, "Sophia's dead, Thomas. I'm sorry."

"What!" Thomas shouted angrily. "My wife died and I wasn't there! You had me helping complete strangers! I should have been with Sophia instead of breaking into plague infected buildings!"

"I'm sorry, Thomas," Sita answered softly. "You're right. Why comfort everyone else if you can't help your own family?"

To his credit, however, it didn't take long for Thomas to realize the truth for himself. He knew Sophia might die even before he left to open the buildings, and Thomas now felt certain that Sita had done all she could. "Come on, Dukka," Thomas said with a feeling of resignation. "We must find a place for Sita to rest."

Thomas and Dukka picked up their dying friend and carried her down the street until they reached an empty basement. Then they gently positioned her on the cold musty floor. Finally, Sita remembered her mystic teacher. "Dharmaji! Dharmaji!" she cried out in desperation. "Where are you?"

When Dharmaji failed to answer Sita's desperate cry for help, Thomas and Dukka couldn't offer her any solace. Her terrible suffering had crushed her courage, and her thoughts quickly turned dark and disjointed. Sita's condition continued to worsen, and since Thomas knew he couldn't ease her mind, he left Dukka alone with her while he departed to bury his wife. When Thomas disappeared down the street, Dukka spoke. "My child, still you don't recognize me?"

Sita gave Dukka a terrified glance. In her suffering and distress, she couldn't comprehend her friend's inexplicable words. Finally, the enigmatic Dukka touched Sita's forehead, and they both transported back to the stream near the outcropping of boulders.

Sita immediately recognized the familiar landscape around her and quickly examined her forehead and neck. Both the fever and nodule had vanished. She then gazed intently at Dukka, and saw him miraculously transform himself into the Great Being known as Dharmaji.

At first, Sita seemed reassured by Dharmaji's presence, but soon she became angry and defensive. "Why did you try to kill me?" Sita demanded. "You told me I needed to learn about life from you. Does that include terrifying me and nearly murdering me?"

Dharmaji remained silent for a while allowing Sita to express her indignation. But he also remained quiet to give her the opportunity to perhaps answer her own question. Finally, he felt compelled to respond to her.

"Sita," he began slowly. "The word 'Dukka' means suffering and it's a part of life. In fact, it isn't possible to learn about suffering without experiencing it yourself. The same is also true of death. It cannot be adequately understood by merely witnessing it in others. It remains a deeply personal experience. But another reason for learning about both suffering and death exists as well. They teach compassion for the suffering of others."

Sita still felt distressed even after hearing the Mystic Teacher's explanation and her anger sounded harsh. "I'm going home now," she asserted bluntly. "I don't wish to learn anything more from you. Besides, I'm already very late, and my family will be worried. This lesson has been a waste of my time."

"Where is time?" Dharmaji asked rhetorically.

Sita departed from the Great One and ran all the way home. When she arrived, she rushed inside the small cottage and hugged her father warmly. He looked at her kindly and declared, "Thanks for feeding the cows and fetching the water. You started your chores before I woke up this morning!"

Her father's remark both surprised and startled Sita. She gazed around the cottage carefully and suddenly realized that she had been gone for only a few hours.

The Enchanted Notebook

Sita felt greatly reassured surrounded by her loving family again, and she experienced a renewed sense of security. Her short, but intense encounter with Dharmaji by the stream, and her strange ordeal in the forest had left her puzzled and frightened, but now these troubles seemed to be behind her. Safely together with her family once more, she enthusiastically attended to her daily chores and allowed herself to relax. Her daily routine provided a powerful source of comfort and support, and her disturbing experiences slowly lost their hold over her. Allowing her memories to fade, Sita embraced her old life as if it felt fresh and exciting.

In addition, Sita also resolved to inform her parents about Dharmaji and his miraculous ability to cure her deafness. Her mother especially deserved to hear the truth, Sita felt; because her mother carried the burden of worry and guilt that she couldn't always conceal from her daughter. Sita also decided to describe her horrifying experiences with the Crimson Plague including her near fatal illness in Galaway.

For about a week, Sita waited patiently for an opportunity to tell her parents when they were alone. At last, one morning, she found them together in the barn gathering straw while her brothers Adam and Jeremy slept in their room. "You're right, mother," Sita began enthusiastically. "Now, I can hear. But I couldn't tell you."

Her parents stopped their work and gazed at their daughter in amazement. Then her mother asked, "Sita, did you say you can hear?"

Sita nodded enthusiastically and then backed about thirty yards away from them. "Say something!" she shouted.

Her father hesitated at first, but then began to recite the letters of the alphabet, but in a random order. Of course, Sita miraculously repeated them all correctly. Sita's mother cried out, "Sita, oh my Sita," and hurried to embrace her. Her father also became very inspired, but he also looked perplexed. "How can this be?" he asked when he understood his daughter could actually hear.

"It's really hard to explain," Sita began. "And it's even more difficult to believe."

"Go on," her mother encouraged. "We need to know."

"All right," Sita replied, drawing a deep breath. "When I went hiking through the forest, I met a Great Being named Dharmaji."

Before Sita could continue, her father interrupted her. "What do the words, "Great Being" signify?"

Sita's mother quickly interrupted him. "Keep still! Let her finish! Go on Sita."

"Anyway," Sita went on. "First, Dharmaji visited me in a kind of dream vision, and then later, I encountered him in person by the giant boulders near the stream behind our farm. While I stood waiting there, he tricked me into disappearing into another world where everyone appeared to be dying or dead."

While Sita continued to relate her highly improbable story, it became clear to her that her parents seemed to be growing confused and frightened. She soon discerned she couldn't tell her parents the truth because, if she did, they might consider her to be mentally unsteady and in need of careful supervision. So, she decided to bend the truth for everyone's sake. "What I'm trying to say," she said meekly, "I had beautiful dream. When I finally woke up, I could hear!"

Sita's parents' expression of relief and elation gave Sita all the evidence she required to understand that her parents had been persuaded. "It's a miracle!" her mother exclaimed. "Who would have thought our little girl could be cured in a dream? It's a miracle!"

Within hours Sita became a noteworthy person in her tiny village. Her father seemed especially proud and repeated the story, embellishing it every time he told it. In addition, Sita could now be herself, and she drank in all the wonderful sounds and songs that now filled her mind and touched her heart.

Nevertheless, despite her good fortune and her best efforts, Sita still couldn't get Dharmaji out of her thoughts. Days drifted into months, but still she replayed the entire plague episode in her mind, in an attempt to put it to rest, so she could move beyond it. However, her experiences had been complicated, and they rendered no clear or simple answers. Just as important, hadn't he come to her in a magic vision? Furthermore, if he represented some kind of evil, how could he heal her and create such a wondrous light?

It became clear after several months of inner turmoil that Sita simply couldn't answer her own questions. She needed to contact Dharmaji if she wished to find the answers she now so earnestly sought.

So, one afternoon, with all these questions directing her steps, Sita approached the meandering stream near her home and sat down. She felt determined to wait for Dharmaji at the exact spot where they had first met. From her vantage point, she could see her parents sitting in front of their thatched cottage oblivious to her movements. The wafting smoke from the stone chimney indicated that her brothers were still napping and her parents would soon be preparing dinner.

As she lingered by the stream, Sita wrote down all the questions she would ask Dharmaji when he appeared and carefully rehearsed each one aloud. While she waited, the time dragged on, however, and her courage and fervor waned. She soon became dejected believing another encounter with Dharmaji seemed highly improbable. Perhaps Sita's last encounter with the mystic being now made her unworthy of his help somehow.

But then he appeared. He looked like such a unique and mysterious being; Sita could have recognized him from a great distance. Yet, the Cosmic Visitor chose to appear directly behind her near the forest pines; and soon he stood beside her.

"Dharmaji!" Sita exclaimed forgetting her carefully crafted questions. "You're really here! I knew you'd come!" Dharmaji's presence both inspired and invigorated Sita, and she felt the thrill of adventure returning.

"Yes," the Mystic Leader answered in a calm resolute voice. "I've come to answer your questions and ask one of my own."

Sita suddenly remembered her notes and decided to ask her two most important questions. "Dharmaji," she asked tentatively. "Why did you actually lead me into those awful places of death and disease when you disguised yourself as Dukka?"

"If you want to travel with me," Dharmaji answered assertively, "you must be aware that suffering is a part of life. It's not possible to truly learn about sorrow without experiencing it, as I have already told you. Since you, and most others, wouldn't actively seek out suffering in order to understand it, I decided to bring it to you. It represented a kind of initiation that was designed to test your courage and patience. By giving you the most difficult challenge first, I'll now be able to teach you more quickly. Instead of assigning you some small, largely inconsequential assignments first, I simply created one very challenging test, so you could prove yourself. Now, ask your other question."

Sita now understood Dharmaji a little better even if she couldn't agree with him. She decided to ask her second question. "Why did you advise me to hide the hearing miracle from my family?"

"You already know the answer," Dharmaji replied slowly. "What happened when you told your parents about me?"

"I think they thought I might be unstable," Sita admitted.

"Yes, if you would've continued relating your honest description," the Secret Mystic continued, "everyone would have ridiculed you or worse. Nevertheless, your clever response about the dream appeared to be quite resourceful. That kind of quick thinking could prove useful in the future. Now, I have a question for you. Why is it you only called for me when you believed you might be dying? Why didn't you seek me out when the others faced death?"

The truth of Dharmaji's statement stung Sita's pride, and she instantly realized the truth. She bowed her head and replied, "Even though I helped others, I didn't treat their suffering as my own. I could have called you at any time and ended all our anguish."

The Great One smiled and realized his trust had been well placed in his young student. "Yes, it is so. Thoughts of selfishness can be extremely subtle and very difficult to overcome. But more importantly, you did learn from your mistake, and you have ultimately managed your fear. It also should be noted that you helped others throughout the entire Crimson Plague episode."

"Sita, to be honest," Dharmaji continued more seriously now. "I need your complete cooperation, and unfortunately your good ideas and noble actions won't be enough even though they remain truly important. Every situation we'll soon encounter will have many unknown dangers requiring a combination of courage, resourcefulness and charity. I must prepare you myself or our mission will fail. It's out of concern and not harshness that motivates me to create these reflective visions."

Sita tried to understand the Great Mystic's strange clarification, and felt inclined to believe him, at least enough to begin to trust him again. She sat in silence for only a few moments, and then with both fear and anticipation, she asked her mysterious teacher about her next task. "I'm ready to try again," she called out, attempting to sound both modest and confident.

Dharmaji felt a sense of solace realizing that Sita might indeed be the one for whom he had been searching. He bent down and picked up her green notebook lying on the ground beside her and tore out all the pages except three. Returning it to her, Sita held the sketchpad in her hands and watched in amazement, as it began to sparkle with an ethereal blue glow. The magic color felt very cool to her touch, and soon began emitting a whirring sound that created a feeling of power. While Sita continued grasping the glowing notebook, Dharmaji touched it with a quick "rap" and the notebook returned to its original color and texture.

Before Sita could recover from her astonishment and ask questions, Dharmaji explained. "Since I crafted your first challenge, I'm giving you the chance to create the second one. Your assignment is to write an original story. It must be started at dawn and completed by sunset. In other words, you must continue writing until you succeed in composing your narrative in a single day."

"Why?" Sita interrupted, already complaining. "Anyone can write a story."

Dharmaji raised his voice sternly and replied, "Your impatience is still a problem. You didn't allow me to finish. This composition won't be just any story. Whatever story you write between the hours of dawn and twilight will become real on the following day."

"I don't understand," Sita said, more respectfully now.

"You must write a three page story," Dharmaji continued authoritatively, "and you must begin to write at dawn and finish by sunset. When the task has been completed the story will come to life the following day."

Having understood her teacher's explanation in more detail, Sita realized that this assignment might be a challenge she would truly enjoy. She would invent the characters and plot herself. She could also compose a "happy ending" that didn't involve death, disease, or despair. She could even make certain no unforeseen forces waited behind rocks and trees.

As she held her enchanted notebook more respectfully now, as if it had become a sacred text or living presence, she still wished to ask her mysterious friend two more important questions. "What if I can't complete the story in a single day?" she asked. "What will happen?"

Dharmaji gazed down at the stream and replied enigmatically, "Then you'll grow old trying."

Only then did Sita understand the importance of her new task beyond its novelty. Her childish thoughts of wish fulfillment seemed naive. She vowed to herself that she needed to write the most hopeful, promising story possible. As she studied the notebook again, it became clear to her that this writing task would be more complicated than she first believed. Like an arrow shot from a bow, it couldn't be recalled once it had been put in motion. This grim realization about her writing task created a feeling of doubt and responsibility within her which she initially hoped she might escape. However, when she looked up to ask the Cosmic Being about her growing apprehension, he had disappeared once again.

A Test of Faith

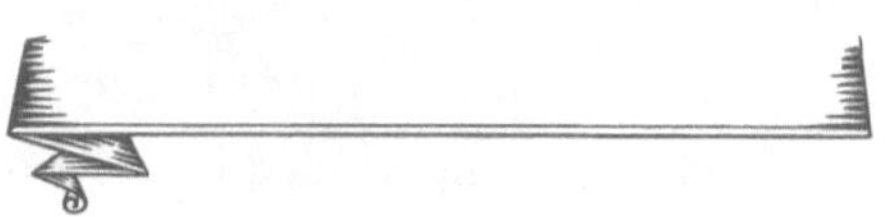

Sita walked home that day feeling a sense of urgency about her unusual writing project. When she entered through the back door, she attempted to project a casual attitude, so she greeted her parents cheerfully. She then climbed up the stairs to her room and hid her notebook among her sweaters in the bottom drawer of her dresser. Later, at dinner, she behaved as if nothing out of the ordinary was happening, and then she returned to her room as soon as she could leave the table without arousing suspicion. That night, as she lay in her bed unable to sleep, her wild and wandering thoughts struggled to create a magical story.

Initially, to be sure, Sita's thoughts betrayed her immaturity. She thought of galloping princes and magnificent castles. She also entertained ideas taken from children's books such as the granting of three wishes and the appearance of a magic carpet. Even still, something deep within kept prompting her to write something more compelling than a simple story that seemed selfish and immature.

Instead, Sita ultimately began to focus her attention on the needs of others. Perhaps she could help the sick, the lonely, or even the dying. She began to consider that Dharmaji would be impressed with her if she could demonstrate a genuine wish to help those in distress. But then another thought began to pull at her. Wasn't the desire to please her teacher just another form of selfishness? Clearly, she remained self-centered if her primary purpose for writing a story was to impress her guide.

This feeling of being limited by the constraints of her childish story ideas left Sita feeling restless and worried until almost daybreak. Frustrated and fatigued, she finally decided to rise early and complete her chores as quickly as prudence would allow. Then she hurried up to her tiny room and retrieved the notebook from its hiding place. After taking a few deep breaths, she centered herself and began to write. Only at lunch time did she decide to take a break. As she read over the first two pages, she felt satisfied that her story seemed to be progressing smoothly and rapidly.

After careful consideration, Sita had resolved to write about the beauty of the natural world around her. Having experienced the pain of suffering and disease, the young writer now wished to describe the more elegant scenes of the transforming seasons. If the world could be harsh sometimes, it could also be beautiful too.

Nonetheless, Sita understood that once she had finished her nature story, she would have to be willing to face both the intended and unintended consequences of her work regardless of her good intentions. Nevertheless, she remained determined. Dharmaji had given her the responsibility of writing a story, and she would faithfully follow his instructions.

The first full day of Sita's writing project went well, but she couldn't finish because she couldn't fashion a character to fit her ideas. The next two days also became frustrating, since her parents needed her to help thatch the roof, weed the vegetable garden, and make supper. Finally, after a number of interruptions and near completions, Sita eventually completed the three page writing task in a single day. Then, as the shadows of evening slowly enveloped her room, she hid the completed story under her pillow and waited eagerly for the rising sun to magically bring her composition to life.

At dawn, the incredible happened. Sita and her family were rudely awakened by a sharp "tap" at the front door. Sita's father quickly vaulted out of bed and responded to the strange knock. When he opened the door, he discovered a sad old man humbly stretching out his withered hand begging for something to eat. Sita then raced to the door and recognized the very being she had written about in her story. She approached him more closely and asked. "Are you Father Time?"

"Yes," he replied weakly. "I'm very old, and very, very tired. I need to rest for a while."

In her innocence, Sita had written herself into her story as a temporary replacement for Father Time. The young writer believed she could portray the wondrous beauty of the seasons through the images in her story. "I'll take charge for a while," she said eagerly. "You can rest by the fire for three days, and then you can take responsibility again."

"Very well," Father Time replied meekly. "If it's all right with you, I'll rest by the fire now."

Just as Sita's story had foretold, her family granted Father Time's request and left the old man alone by the fire after he had eaten. This gave Sita the chance to assume her primary roles as writer and director. She stepped outside with the purity of good intentions and the predicament of poor judgment, and began to transform the season of summer into winter. The young creator raised her arms and began to powder the willows and pines with white fluffy snow. She then froze the meandering stream into a sheet of transparent ice that glowed in the sun. She even cloaked the cottages and streets with a thick layer of beautiful crystal snowflakes.

Not surprisingly, the unsuspecting villagers felt stunned by the drastic change of the landscape around them, and at first, they felt awestruck. The wondrous display of natural forces seemed like a miracle. But before long, the sobering reality of their situation began to take hold. Every part of their natural world appeared to be either sleeping or dying. The vegetables and fruits began freezing on the vines and trees. The frigid wind also swept over them where they stood, so they worriedly gathered firewood and sought shelter from the storm.

But that wasn't the worst of it. Sita's brothers, Adam and Jeremy, had accidentally fallen into a deep pool in the village stream at the exact moment it had frozen, and now they both lay motionless at the bottom.

By the time Sita realized that her brothers could be in deadly peril, she became understandably alarmed. She raced to find her notebook to discover what had happened, but felt horrified when she realized it was missing. She searched everywhere until, at last, she figured out what probably happened. She assumed her brothers must have stolen the notebook while they were snooping in her room. They then undoubtedly scribbled something down while she kept busy with her chores.

She bolted into their room, found the story book, and turned to the back cover. There two stick figures with her brothers' names, Adam and Jeremy, appeared scrawled at the bottom. It seemed from the drawing that her brothers needed to hold their breath beneath the surface of the frozen pool.

Now Sita really needed to tell her parents the truth. She searched for them in a complete panic, until finally she found them in the barn. She tried hysterically to explain the crisis including the powerful magic notebook. She also blurted out the details about the life threatening condition her brothers now faced imprisoned in the frozen stream. She even showed them the stick figure drawings on the bottom of the notebook itself.

Unfortunately, her parents didn't understand her. "What are you talking about, Sita?" her mother asked. "You don't have any brothers. Show your father your book."

Her father seemed unconcerned as well. "You know you are an only child, Sita. But it would be nice if you had a couple of brothers, wouldn't it? Now, help your mother bring in some firewood; this blizzard is getting worse."

"Oh, no!" Sita gasped, finally realizing her terrible mistake. "I forgot to write Adam and Jeremy into my story, so they decided to write themselves into it anyway. What have I done?"

Sita tried desperately to gain control over her racing thoughts and endeavored to consider the situation more rationally. She then suddenly remembered, Father Time, sleeping by the fire at home. She ran inside but when she approached him, he looked so deeply asleep that he might be impossible to wake. As her panic intensified, she rushed outside and attempted to return the winter season to summer but failed. Her story required three days of winter, and it now happened to be the first afternoon. The young author now felt frightened beyond all consolation, even as her parents attempted to make sense of their daughter's strange conversation and behavior.

At last, the terrified girl shouted out for Dharmaji; so he could break the spell, but this time he didn't respond. She called for him repeatedly until finally she comprehended, she would have to restore the situation herself. Then, like a miracle, the truth about the crisis finally eased her tortured mind. In two days, everything would return to the way it had been. All she needed to do was to stay patient and wait.

Sita's conclusion seemed plausible, but time passed with an agonizing slowness that kept her in a perpetual state of doubt and fear. When she finally saw the sunrise on the third day, the whole experience seemed like some awful nightmare. She rushed into her brothers' room and found them peacefully sleeping. She could find no evidence of harm to either of them and neither could she find Father Time. She also felt greatly relieved that her parents didn't know of her exceedingly poor judgment.

With gratitude and relief, Sita sprinted out to the village stream where she and Dharmaji had met and tucked the troublesome notebook safely under her arm. Several hours later the great teacher appeared, but he seemed very disappointed. "That seemed like an odd story you wrote," he said sternly. "Did you deliberately leave your brothers out?"

"No, Dharmaji," Sita stammered. "I didn't want them to get hurt. But I guess I mostly just forgot about them."

"Yes," Dharmaji replied. "If I hadn't remained with them for those three days, they would've perished."

"I don't understand." Sita answered, suddenly anxious again. "My story lasted three days and then it ended."

"That's true," the Cosmic Visitor asserted. "But just because your story lasted three days doesn't mean those specific days didn't exist at all. Reality is much more complicated than you realize."

"I still don't understand," the girl spoke in confusion.

"I needed to restore everything you altered as if it never occurred," Dharmaji responded. "But I wanted you to experience the consequences of your lack of self-discipline in writing about things that affect others."

Sita finally started to understand. "Does that mean you were Father Time in my story?" she asked.

"I am part of everyone and everything," Dharmaji answered. "It's important to remember that nothing stands alone. Everything in the world affects everything else. You must remember that it's important to consider what you've left out of your life, as well as what you've included in it. Your brothers represent good example of this principle. In addition, you neglected to consider how your story might affect the villagers."

Sita remained exhausted from her ordeal and simply desired rest and forgiveness from Dharmaji. Although she had made mistakes, they weren't deliberate.

The mystic teacher's face softened a bit, seeing his student struggling, "Remember child, mistakes, even innocent ones, can be dangerous and even deadly. Even good intentions can lead to disaster."

"Yes," Sita replied, grateful that Dharmaji still cared for her. She carefully returned the notebook to the Eternal One, clearly relieved to be free of the responsibility.

But instead of accepting it, Dharmaji tapped the notebook, allowed the story to dissolve, and returned it to her saying, "Try again, child."

The Final Audition

At first, Sita seemed unwilling to even consider another writing project that Dharmaji had now proposed. The very thought of writing another unpredictable narrative frightened her. "I will not," she uttered in a tone that revealed both anger and apprehension. You told me yourself that I didn't write a useful story."

"I disagree," the wise mystic replied with a measure of understanding in his voice. "The story may not have helped others, but it did help you to better understand yourself and the world around you."

Sita still didn't feel inclined to be persuaded by her teacher's attempt to get her to participate in yet another assessment. These tests meant to be preparing her for some vague mission seemed pointless and even cruel. But again, Dharmaji surprised her. "This will be your final challenge. This world is in desperate need of our service, so I've been required to teach you as quickly and intensely as possible. I apologize for your rather harsh treatment, but it couldn't be avoided."

The young girl became more willing to listen to Dharmaji's words, but she still felt badly shaken, and she vividly remembered her failures. But a moment later, Sita expressed a revelation of her own. "I'll write another story," she began, "if I can cast you as a main character. Then, whenever I need you, you'll be right beside me."

The old man admired his student's growing shrewdness and attention to detail. With him by her side, Dharmaji knew that Sita assumed that the plot and themes of her story would be far less likely to twist and turn in dangerous directions. He wanted to grant her request, but he added one more condition.

"If I'm going to travel with you, your story must be filled with real risks and challenges, otherwise it will not teach you anything worth learning. Our mission is about to begin, so finish your story quickly. Then, I can reveal to you my identity and the purpose of our journey. Now go, child, and return soon."

As Sita returned to her family cottage, Adam and Jeremy could be seen playing in the yard, while her parents kept busy in the field. Almost instinctively, she grabbed a hoe and joined her parents in their work still musing about her teacher's mysterious remarks. She'd been badly frightened twice, and yet she still agreed to another difficult assignment. She had also detected sense urgency in his voice that sounded both eerie and disturbing.

Nevertheless, the young student also felt a profound sense of duty toward Dharmaji and his mission. She decided to draft the story as quickly as possible. This sense of responsibility included planning the plot carefully with no childish mistakes. Only then could she be certain that her chances for success would be greatly enhanced.

It seemed that even Providence itself might be guiding Sita as well. Her parents and twin brothers had scheduled a visit to her mother's friend overnight, and Sita's parents needed her to complete all the chores while they were away. This fortunate circumstance would allow the young writer to work at the kitchen table all day and finish the chores during short breaks. By the time her family departed a few hours later, Sita acted so enthusiastically that she nearly pushed them out the front door.

Finally alone, Sita took out the mysterious notebook from her new hiding place behind the kitchen cupboard and began to write. She recorded her thoughts all day stopping just long enough to work on her chores. By twilight, she had accomplished her task. Sita felt so tired and the story so occupied her mind that she nodded off to sleep while resting her head on the kitchen table. At dawn, she heard a cryptic knock on the door, when Sita opened it , she yelled, "Dharmaji you're here!"

"Yes, Sita, I'm with you now. So, let's begin your story. It's called "the Wizard Girl of Waterville" is it not?"

"Yes," the writer beamed. "I think you'll like it!"

The two companions, student and master, left the cottage and walked toward the winding village stream near the woods. When they reached its banks, they hiked around a bend, along a narrow shoreline and then, unexpectedly, the entire countryside seemed utterly transformed. The sky now appeared to be filled with dark ominous clouds, and the ground appeared saturated by a cold driving rain. The rain fell relentlessly with only a few rays of sunlight able to penetrate the massive cloud cover above them.

As they continued on their way along the river bank, Dharmaji and Sita ultimately reached a tiny village with about two dozen structures. They appeared to be businesses, local government offices, and small residential dwellings. Almost no one walked on the street, and the atmosphere felt as cold and uninviting as the weather.

Seeking to escape the downpour, Dharmaji and Sita ducked inside a nearby general store. They introduced themselves to the proprietor, who stood behind a long wooden counter. Surprisingly, the solitary man responded with neither warmth nor civility. Instead, the arrogant fellow appeared to be totally indifferent to their every attempt at friendly conversation. Furthermore, when Sita discreetly glanced over at the other patrons in the store, she observed that they seemed to be equally unfriendly as well. Their accusing eyes and angry scowls made Sita feel like a criminal.

Sita, of course, anticipated this unfriendly encounter from her story, but its intensity surprised her. She began to worry about the merits of her story as it was now unfolding. Still, Sita decided to allow the plot to unfold as she had carefully written it. She waited patiently near the counter for a few minutes longer, and then she observed an old woman hobbling into the shop.

The aged woman looked frail, and bent over, with cold piercing eyes. Intent upon examining every item in the shop, the old woman began wandering down every aisle, making the owner and other customers very uneasy. Before long, these patrons became so genuinely intimidated by the old woman's presence, they began exiting the shop as quickly and discreetly as possible.

As Sita continued to study the old woman lurking around the aisles, she began to identify more of her character's traits from her story. In addition to the old woman's strange appearance and intense gaze, she also mumbled angrily to herself as if cursing at someone or something. This spectacle suggested a sense of mental unpredictability that appeared to be both suspicious and dangerous.

The old woman continued this odd behavior for the entire time she limped through the shop, as she picked up various items, and then tossed them back down. Eventually, she chose some vegetables and fruit, and then left the place as menacingly as she had arrived. After she left, the customers quickly reentered the shop and began cursing the old woman under their breath, so no one else could hear.

Sita took Dharmaji aside and quietly explained the situation to him, believing he might be unaware of the details of their strange encounter. "That old woman has put a curse on the village, so that it rains, all day every day. Because of the constant storms, the villagers remain completely dependent on the outside world for their survival. Everything they need that requires sunlight must be carried over the mountains, and even though the villagers despise this terrible place, they are also afraid to leave it. The village is surrounded by mountains, deserts, and even an ocean. Anyone who has attempted to leave has never been heard from again."

"Are you saying this town has never seen the sun?" Dharmaji asked sounding surprised.

"Almost never," Sita replied. "There's barely enough sunlight for them to survive. The old hag has cursed this village infecting it with fear and despair. The villagers despise the old witch, but they also fear her. The crisis has continued for many years. As a consequence, everything the people do is designed to endure the weather and avoid the witch. The people have become weary after all this time, and need relief."

"So what are you planning to do?" Dharmaji asked curiously.

"I must do away with the dreaded old woman and save the village from their fate," Sita continued. "Remember Dharmaji, you specifically told me to pick a difficult confrontation."

"I see," the Great Being replied with seemingly more uncertainty now. "So, what will you do?"

"The old woman has a magic book of spells that she hides behind her fireplace mantel. She uses it to create the rain, and I'm going to sneak into her shack and steal the book. Then I'm going to reverse the spells, and rescue the village."

"So you haven't memorized the words to the specific incantations yet?" Dharmaji wanted to know.

"No," Sita replied almost condescendingly. "It wouldn't be any challenge at all if I knew all the spells ahead of time."

Dharmaji comprehended that the girl seemed convinced of her ability, so he didn't discuss the spell book any longer. He did, however, ask about the witch herself. "What will you do with the old woman?"

Sita smiled knowingly as if she had just outsmarted her mentor and guide. "That will be your job," she said definitively. "You must subdue the old woman, so I can steal the secret spell book."

Of course, the Mystic Leader already knew all about Sita's plot, nevertheless, it provided a real test of her compassion and strength. He asked himself, "*Would Sita actually want me to vanquish the old woman and end her life, or would she desire me to spare her? Would she even be able to end the curse by learning the spells correctly?*"

At this point Dharmaji decided to follow rather than lead. "When do you want me to get rid of the old woman?" the Cosmic Being asked. "And how do you want me to accomplish it?"

"We will approach her shack this afternoon while there is at least a little daylight," Sita replied with a commanding voice. "Take care of her in whatever way you think will be the most persuasive."

"No," Dharmaji replied assertively. "I will not."

"Why not?" Sita blurted out, suddenly feeling nervous and less self-assured.

"Find out for yourself," her teacher replied dryly.

Sita quickly recovered her sense of humility and poise and responded to the mystic teacher's uninspiring tone. "Something is wrong. Dharmaji, what mistake am I making? You promised to help me."

The Cosmic Visitor paused a moment and then explained, "I'll distract the old woman long enough for you to steal the spell book, but that is all. I won't kidnap her, nor will I do away with her as you seem to suggest."

"Thank you, Dharmaji," the girl exclaimed in relief. "You're right. I overreacted when I made plans to injure the old woman. It won't happen again. Now, I'm ready."

After their somewhat strained discussion ended, the two sojourners hiked toward the old woman's hovel which stood far from the village near the mountain foothills. When they arrived, they could easily discern an old dilapidated cottage with holes in the roof that made it look uninhabitable. As they spied on the shack from a discreet distance, it wasn't long before Dharmaji could see the old woman walking around inside the primitive dwelling. They approached closer, and then the Mystic Teacher kept his promise by luring the old woman outside by making peculiar animal sounds.

When the old woman finally vacated the shack, Sita quickly dashed inside and grabbed the spell book from its hiding place behind the mantel. Then she escaped outside through the back door feeling empowered by her victory.

Then, completely unexpectedly, the old woman reappeared and began pursuing Sita as best as her frail body would permit. In her haste, the old witch accidentally tripped over a tree root and tumbled head long to the ground. By the time Sita and Dharmaji found the elderly woman and figured out what had happened, she seemed unconscious or worse.

Miraculously, however, the rain ceased. The storm clouds parted and the sun burst through an open sky. Sita smiled happily realizing that her story had a cheerful ending at last, despite the old woman's predicament. Her mystic teacher's unforeseen actions had altered her story somewhat, but now the rains had ended anyway. As can be imagined, the town spent the rest of the day in joyful celebration.

Sita strolled regally through the town and thoroughly reveled in the adulation of the wonderstruck villagers who continually waved to her and gleefully danced in the street. Before long, the bloated sewers and overflowing reservoirs were rapidly draining out. The sun began to awaken the entire town and, for the first time in one hundred years, there existed a sense of renewed hope and purpose.

However, even while the sun continued to beat down on the third day, the unimaginable happened. From deep within the earth, intense heat began to rise up through the still soggy ground creating steam and countless fires all over the village. Within hours, the entire town became inundated with smoke so thick that it appeared impossible for the citizens to escape it. While the flames leapt from the ground to the buildings, every living inhabitant proved to be at risk. Watching in horror, Sita finally apprehended that the old woman's rain spells were meant to hold back the violent heat and flames, before they could break through the water logged ground.

In a state of frenzied panic, Sita began searching through the spell book desperately searching for the right incantations that would bring back the rains. Her terror grew so intense, however, it nearly paralyzed her. All she could read were blurred words on indecipherable pages. Meanwhile, the fires raged on, and soon the town became completely engulfed by the blaze. This forced the villagers to either flee in panic toward the seashore or attempt to escape through the mountain foothills. Sita looked on in disbelief and shame while she clutched the useless spell book.

As the disaster rapidly descended into chaos, the Cosmic Visitor wisely determined to end the story and release Sita from its horrible climax. Within the time it takes to awaken from a nightmare, they both had returned to the village stream near Sita's house. The fires had now disappeared, but the horrific memory remained.

Sita's sense of failure and disgrace seemed to be almost unbearable, as she attempted to explain herself to her teacher. But he stopped her abruptly. "That was the final test," Dharmaji asserted impatiently. "If that story had been truly real, you would have disrupted an entire world and endangered the lives of every living person in that defenseless village. Now the testing has ended; prepare to leave home at dawn."

But by now, Sita felt utterly devastated. No longer willing to follow the mystic leader, she spoke her mind without reservation even while the tears rolled down her cheeks. "No, Dharmaji," she shouted out miserably. "I'm no longer worthy to follow you. I consistently make costly mistakes that will bring only misery to me and to everybody else. You must realize that yourself by now. No matter how carefully I plan and no matter how thoughtfully I act, it never works out. Please leave me alone. I won't be persuaded to follow you again."

The Cosmic Visitor expected this response from his student and he prepared to answer. "I made you fail," he replied candidly. "You needed to experience the town's destruction. In fact, I made certain that you would be defeated. It was I who cornered the old woman and brought the inferno. You simply didn't have the chance to succeed."

Now, Sita felt angry. "What do you mean? Are you suggesting that you deliberately caused me to lose control of my own story?"

"Yes," Dharmaji answered simply.

"Why would you do that?" she complained. "You always make me miserable. Even after all my careful planning, I still fail terribly. Other than that I've learned nothing."

The Great Being listened patiently and then continued with his explanation. "We learn little from success except ambition. However, from defeat we learn patience. I needed to teach you how to bear sorrow and defeat because soon we will be immersed in them. The struggling world has a great need for our help at this time, and I needed to prepare you. The forces of darkness are now in danger of crowding out the power of the light. The time has come to shoulder the wheel of love and truth, so the way of darkness will be expelled from the villages and pushed back beyond the mountains.

"The world continues to be staggering under the weight of poverty, injustice, and greed. It's stumbling toward the abyss in selfishness and despair. In order to succeed, we must be willing to bear defeat and disappointment until we become successful enough to remind the world of the sun within us all. We cannot ultimately save the world from darkness entirely, but we can drive it back far, so the inner light will re-energize the world once more. No setback or defeat will vanquish us if we remember why we face the enemy."

Sita, once again, felt baffled by the Great Being's words. But, even still, it did matter to her that she was actually meant to lose control of her story. Since it proved impossible for her to succeed, then, in fact, she hadn't really failed after all. This idea provided Sita with a little solace and reassurance, at least, even though her nerves remained badly frayed.

"Tomorrow," Dharmaji went on. "Our journey will begin in earnest. We will sojourn to the Gonald River above the Enila Falls, and then we will trek high into the Dhala Mountains. In these secret and remote expanses, we will search for my friends. After we locate these allies, we will attempt to capture and hold the notorious fortress city of Graganite which rules over the region beyond the Dhala Mountains."

Sita felt stunned by the mystic leader's statement. "Are you going to overthrow the Kingdom of Sutin?"

Dharmaji answered simply and directly. "Sutin's father once lived as a generous king, but his son has become ruthless and ambitious. He has begun a campaign to outlaw individual freedoms, even as he taxes the poor and starves his subjects. The population will soon be decimated if we don't intervene. The darkness has taken hold there, at Sutin's castle. We must terminate Sutin's reign of brutality and indifference before all hope is extinguished."

Sita now understood more fully the reasons for her harsh initiation and training. She suspected Dharmaji knew that the mission would be extraordinarily difficult, and she recognized his toughness as a way of teaching her self-discipline and meaningful service. Nevertheless, she still felt uncertain whether she would be willing to follow the Cosmic Visitor, especially since she still questioned her own abilities. "Dharmaji, I don't think I can do this," she said sadly.

This timid assertion did not resonate well with Dharmaji who seemed unwilling to coddle his wavering student. Instead, his mood became harsh and challenging.

"Child," he began, "It's time to make a decision. I've answered your many complaints and addressed your every insecurity. There's no more time to waste on your doubts and fears. The starving people of Sutin's realm now face desperation. Their terrible cries echo down the mountains and through the meadows. It's time to begin. We must advance quickly now. So we've no time to say goodbye to your family and friends. If we succeed, you will meet up with them again. If we don't, they will have been conquered, and we will be dead."

Of course, the Great Leader's statements seemed brutally candid to the point of cruelty. He also seemed to have presented Sita with many ideas and emotions that she couldn't possibly have understood in such a short space of time. Nevertheless, she believed at least, some of the strange things he had related to her. In the end, Sita understood that she really had no choices at all. Dharmaji discerned her village would soon be attacked, and she couldn't allow invaders to destroy her family and village if she could prevent it.

But a part of her still didn't trust her Mystic Teacher either. He had consistently led her to believe an event would occur, and then something else entirely would unfold. She almost always believed in him because of her own inner vision and his command over every situation, yet she also doubted his veracity at times, and this filled her with doubt and uneasiness.

Overall, however, Sita felt inclined to believe that Dharmaji could be someone extraordinary despite her concerns about his deceptions. She also somehow dimly comprehended that the world could indeed be threatened by some evil, if only because Dharmaji himself had the power to draw upon forces to confront it. This included his ability to manipulating events by creating frightening plot alterations in her stories. It also seemed apparent that her mother, father, and brothers could soon be in mortal danger as well. There might be no other way for her to help rescue them if she left Dharmaji's side now.

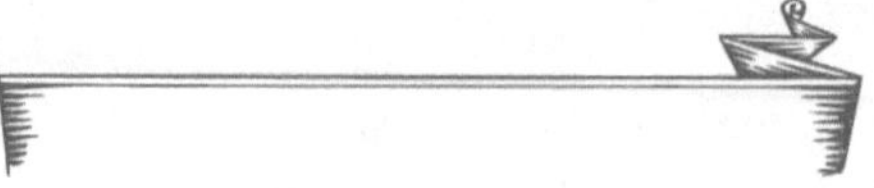

Dharmaji Finds an Ally

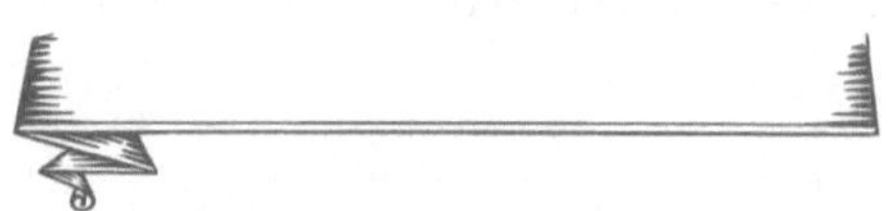

By nightfall, Dharmaji and Sita had journeyed a number of miles upstream where the Sequoia forests of Antolay soon dominated the landscape. Despite the growing shadows of twilight all around, the Great Being knew precisely where to trek and advanced up the stream easily. Sita, however, acted far more tentatively, and she followed Dharmaji so closely, she sometimes bumped up against his heels. She scurried behind him nervously, listening to all the strange and haunting sounds of the Antolay forest. Her heart raced whenever she heard a rustling tree branch or sudden splash from the stream. At times even Dharmaji hesitated briefly and listened intently to the mysterious woodland sounds. Finally, when the darkness had enveloped the entire surrounding wood, the distant moon served as their only lamp.

After several miles, Sita felt exhausted and began lagging behind. Dharmaji didn't seem to notice her condition, but then, at last, he uttered the words she so desperately yearned to hear. "Hurry up. We're nearly there."

This assurance of impending success bolstered the girl's spirits, and she quickly caught up to her teacher. Before long they arrived at a small clearing surrounded by gigantic Sequoia trees and dense vegetation. Dharmaji paused a moment to make certain the location was accurate, and then called up to the natural canopy of tree limbs and creepers above him. Within a few minutes, a huge being swooped down from the trees and glided to the ground.

"Dharmaji!" the flying being exclaimed. "At last, you've come!"

"Yes, Deudal, we meet again, my friend," Dharmaji replied warmly.

Sita appeared spellbound as she stared at the giant flying creature. He had the face of a young mortal but the body of a colossal bird. His brown appearance reassembled the surrounding forest, and his dark green wings looked majestic. His very presence created an image of nobility and power. Witnessing Sita's surprise, Dharmaji introduced her to his friend. "This is Deudal," the Great Leader began. "He represents the last of the Treeganaut race. Deudal has agreed to help us in our approaching conflict with Sutin."

"Yes," Deudal replied. "Sutin and his armies attacked our Antolay Forests many years ago and enslaved my entire nation. I haven't seen any of them in a very long time now, and I fear they've been murdered for their mystic talons."

"I don't understand," Sita inquired as politely as she could. "Why did Sutin wish to murder your friends and steal their claws?"

Dharmaji tried to interrupt the inquisitive girl, but Deudal waved him aside and continued. "Our talons are not simply appendages like those of other birds. They possess a glowing blue liquid and have miraculous curative powers. If someone becomes fatally ill or wounded, the blue fluid will revive him."

Sita thought for a moment and then pressed on. "Mr. Deudal, is it possible someone could live indefinitely if they saved enough blue liquid?"

"Perhaps," the birdman responded. "It remains my belief that Sutin intends to steal all the blue liquid of my people, so he can stay alive for an extended period of time."

"Is that possible?" Sita replied in disbelief.

"Yes," Deudal answered shortly. "Sutin will become more reckless and powerful if he continues to ingest the mystic substance. He may even use it to revive prisoners he wishes to interrogate. He could also employ the remedy as a reward for those who risk their lives for him."

"Then he really must be wicked!" Sita reacted in horror. "So, how do we stop him?"

"My people treasure the glowing blue essence, and we will not surrender it even if we're captured and tortured," Deudal answered sadly.

Suddenly Sita realized intuitively what Deudal and Dharmaji already knew. "You're immortal, aren't you, Deudal?"

"You're right, Thought Healer," Deudal said, turning to Dharmaji. "This child sounds intelligent."

Sita's rush of self-confidence and pride became apparent until Dharmaji answered dryly, "Sometimes she shows signs of discernment."

Notwithstanding Dharmaji's remark, some of Sita's excitement remained. She persisted in questioning the Treeganaut. "If your people exist as immortals, aren't they protected from Sutin's warriors?"

"Unfortunately not," Deudal replied gravely. "There exists one way to end even an immortal's life."

Sita became so curious now that she couldn't stop herself. "Then, how can you die?"

"If I reveal the secret to you," the birdman answered, "you'll know, and you'll tell."

An Alliance Is Forged

It seemed clear from Deudal's ominous remarks there could be some significant reason he didn't choose to answer Sita's intrusive question. Respecting his wish to deflect her curiosity, she decided to let the matter drop, at least, temporarily.

Meanwhile, Dharmaji and Deudal, becoming more thoughtful as the evening progressed, built a modest campfire, and gathered some fruits and tubers. Before long, Dharmaji and Deudal began discussing their plans for the days ahead, and Sita, although sore and weary listened intently.

"We must journey to Riverwood by tomorrow evening," the birdman asserted. "We need to find our companion, Atmun, before he advances into the Dhala Mountains. If we don't, he may attempt to conquer the Sutin Empire alone, and he will most certainly fail."

"But Riverwood must be nearly thirty miles from here," Dharmaji pointedly observed. "The child will never be able to walk that far!"

The word 'child' annoyed Sita especially since she had already learned and experienced so much. Yet, she also agreed that thirty miles would be an almost impossible distance for her to walk in a single day. How could she possibly hike a full day and night with little chance to rest? Sita wanted to speak up and sound brave, but she knew from experience that exaggerating her abilities could get her into trouble; so she kept silent.

However, just when a feeling of dejection had begun to confront the group, Deudal let out a hearty laugh. Turning to the Eternal Being, he said, "Have you forgotten, Dharmaji? I can fly!"

Before Dharmaji could reply, the birdman suddenly grabbed Sita by her backpack and swept her up into the clear blue sky. As Deudal flew ever higher, Sita gradually overcame her initial terror and soon felt familiar with Deudal's movements, as they ascended through the air. By the time they landed, everyone understood the meaning of Deudal's demonstration. The gigantic birdman could easily carry Sita above the treetops whenever she grew weary. It seemed like a perfect solution for Sita's inability to traverse such a distance on foot.

The next morning and with a renewed sense of hope, the three companions advanced upstream rapidly. When Sita appeared to be too tired to continue, Deudal picked her up and set her down further up the trail. Then they would both wait for Dharmaji to rendezvous with them ahead on the path. As they lingered on the path, Sita felt free to ask Deudal questions about the mission. She especially wanted to know about Atmun. "Will Atmun be able to help us?" Sita asked quietly.

Deudal didn't speak at first, but when he did speak, his words, had an air of humility and respect. "Atmun is the wisest and possibly the oldest being in the entire kingdom. He has survived in the foothills of the Dhala Mountains for many, many years. But he may be the saddest being in the realm as well."

"Why is that?" Sita interjected. "If he is so wise, then why isn't he happy or at least content?"

"Because," Deudal replied more forcefully, "Atmun has been bewitched by a spell that he can't break. He's been cursed with the ability to assume any identity except that of his true self."

Sita looked bewildered by Deudal's explanation. "Are you saying, Atmun can change into any being he chooses except his real one?"

"Yes," Deudal replied softly. "Atmun can't discover his true identity except at the moment of his death. This is the burden he must carry."

"How does he know that he will discover his identity even at his death?" Sita persisted.

"He doesn't know for sure," Deudal replied. "But that remains his belief. Otherwise, he would surely despair. If Atmun doesn't recognize his own true self, even at death, then how can he ever solve the mystery of his life?"

Before they could finish their discussion, the Great Mystic came jogging up the path. Catching up to Sita and Deudal, he took a swig from his turtle shell canteen, and they all resumed their hike along the fast moving stream.

By the time they reached Riverwood, Dharmaji proved to be the most exhausted. He collapsed under a large tree branch that overlooked an old rustic town. He took a number of deep cleansing breaths. After resting several minutes, he recovered enough strength to get to his feet. He then scanned the village cottages for some time until he identified the specific dwelling he needed to find. At last, he pointed to a small hut at the far edge of Riverwood and exclaimed, "There's Atmun's house! Come, we must hurry!"

However, even as they prepared to hike down the embankment and cross the meadow into the town below, Atmun himself appeared before them. He simply stepped in front of them on the trail from behind a tall oak tree. The three travelers seemed shocked and silent at first, but soon they recovered their composure. "How did you find us?" Dharmaji asked with a feeling of humor and camaraderie in his voice.

Atmun began to laugh as well, "Your birdman friend continually popped up over the trees. A child could have followed him."

Deudal became more serious while he considered the implications of Atmun's seemingly lighthearted remark. Perhaps if Atmun recognized him flying over the treetops, then maybe Sutin's scouts could have seen him as well. He smiled weakly at his wise old friend, but the three companions silently realized that they might encounter the enemy soon.

Of course, Sita remained unaware of any immediate danger, so she focused on Atmun's strange appearance. He indeed looked old with misshapen limbs and a raspy voice. He also seemed nervous and weak. However, when Atmun noticed Sita's critical glance, he instantly transformed himself into a dashing young knight. Then he asked sarcastically, "Do you prefer this image instead?"

Sita felt startled and didn't know how to respond. She had no idea that Atmun knew what she had been thinking. Finally, she asked, "Did you read my mind? Do you know my thoughts?"

"Yes," Atmun answered with a grin. "At your impressionable age, the thoughts appeared written all over your face!"

The three adults laughed uproariously at Sita's naïve comment and she blushed. She recognized that, at the moment, she remained defenseless, and she felt more vulnerable than ever. Luckily, the Mystic Teacher redirected the conversation in a more sobering direction before Sita felt completely humiliated. "We'll need one more ally," the Great Being interjected. "We can't hope to defeat Sutin at Graganite without at least one more companion. We need Minerva."

"Yes," Deudal nodded in agreement. "The great enchantress from the high Dhala Mountains will certainly help us if she knows our plans."

Not surprisingly, Atmun completely agreed with his comrades. "Yes, Minerva will come. She vehemently opposes the reign of Sutin as much as any of us."

Sita who was listening intently seemed more intrigued as the discussion expanded. "Who's Minerva and why do we need her?"

It fell upon Dharmaji to explain to Sita about the mystic conjurer.

"Minerva has proven to be the most brilliant occultist in the entire world. She has the ability to create visions by altering perceptions of the past, present, and future. She can also find and follow any kind of trail regardless of the circumstances. However, her most miraculous power is her ability to exist simultaneously in two different places at once."

Deudal listened respectfully to Dharmaji until he finished, and then agreed, "Having Minerva with us would be the perfect choice for the last member of our team."

"I agree as well," Atmun interjected again, endorsing the notion.

Now it seemed once again that Sita stood in the metaphorical dark. "How can five individuals defeat an entire army?" she complained.

Sita's remark quickly drew a response from her teacher, Dharmaji. "We seek to avoid an all-out war, because it would create misery and death for scores of innocent people. In the chaos of an enormous conflict, even your brothers may be required to fight for your village's survival."

At this point, Deudal interrupted, attempting to help the young volunteer understand Dharmaji's words in a less abrasive manner. "Sita," he stated to her kindly. "We'll have an army of our own. I'll be our air corps; Dharmaji will be our infantry and Atmun will be our scout. When we locate Minerva, we'll have our artillery battery. The world deceives us, right now. Sutin and his hoard remain extremely dangerous, but they think and move with pride, greed, and savagery, so they will be somewhat predictable in their actions. Even their cruelty and cunning has a certain logic and underlying pattern. In addition, we'll also have the elements of uncertainty and surprise as important capabilities."

It became obvious to young Sita that these beings she called friends must be capable of magnificent feats of courage and strength. Nevertheless, she still hadn't any idea how she could possibly fit into this highly gifted group. She knew there would be something she would be required to accomplish; the three tests of initiation administered by Dharmaji seemed proof enough of that, but she still didn't understand what her real duties might be. This uncertainty, together with her past failures made the likelihood of her succeeding seem remote.

Now with only one member of the team to locate, the growing expeditionary force approached the main trailhead at the foothills of the Dhala Mountains. Their jovial manner continued to help them forward, and Sita drew strength from their calm sense of self-assurance. As the trail grew steeper and began to wind around the side of the mountains, the ascent became more treacherous. The group climbed relentlessly higher as the sunlight began to fade.

To her credit, Sita refused to be treated like a weakling and tried her best to keep pace with the others. She didn't cry out or complain even when she caught her boot on a rock and nearly stumbled off the side of the mountain. Despite Sita's difficulties, she also refused Deudal's unspoken help, and she continued climbing.

Nevertheless, the Mystic Being comprehended Sita's unspoken distress and abruptly demanded that they all stop to rest periodically without mentioning the reason. Sita knew the truth, of course, and she felt grateful.

At one of these rest intervals on the mountain, they finally discovered Minerva, the very being they had been seeking out. Standing on an outcropping of rock high above them, she spoke in a loud booming voice that they recognized instantly.

"Why do you search for me?" she demanded harshly.

"But you already know," Atmun shouted back.

The great enchantress stood motionless on the rocks for several moments, obviously reading the thoughts of all the mountaineers. She rose higher in the sky and shouted, "Meet me at Emerald Lake near the mountain summit. Be there tomorrow at sunset, or you won't meet me at all!"

The mysterious specter then vanished as suddenly as she had appeared, and the group of companions stood alone to explain Minerva's motives on their own. Dharmaji seemed less inclined to question the strange warning than the others were, so he simply took the lead farther up the mountain trail. The others followed maintaining their faith in the Great Being's intuition, but their doubts about Minerva's ultimatum felt unsettling to them.

Unfortunately, even the weather seemed to conspire against them, as they slowly persevered with their ascent. The freezing wind and stinging snow grew so harsh that even Deudal couldn't endure its ferocity. In a moment of uncharacteristic weakness, he nearly surrendered to the blizzard. At last, he cried out, "This wind is too dangerous, it's freezing my wings. They're so heavy I can barely keep them from dragging in the snow."

Sita, who now walked right behind him, also felt badly frightened and completely exhausted. In fact, the entire group appeared to be in trouble, and they faced a life or death decision. They either needed to descend the Dhala Mountain trail immediately, or seek shelter somewhere nearby before the darkness left them completely unprotected.

With the howling wind swirling around them, they shouted to each other in an attempt to devise a plan. Their situation rapidly deteriorated and with no natural shelters in view, they reluctantly decided to retreat back down the mountain. By the time they'd descended halfway down, their bodies felt numb and their nerves were strained.

The group grew exhausted and disappointed when they finally reached a resting place after their dangerous descent. They felt betrayed by Minerva, yet it seemed an impossible inference to make based on their enduring friendship with her. At last, Deudal spoke the words that the rest of the group had been thinking. "Why would Minerva give us an impossible task to accomplish, and why would she appear so cruel?"

At that precise moment, Sita provided her first truly helpful insight. "Maybe Minerva knows of some danger at Emerald Lake, and she acted harshly in order to discourage us. "Has Minerva ever spoken to you so angrily before today?"

"No, never," Atmun answered quickly. "She's always been kind, loving, and even mischievous. Perhaps she attempts to protect us by creating a challenge beyond our capabilities. Sita has made an important point. Now I wonder if Minerva had more than one audience when she stood shouting down at us."

The Mystic Leader, who saw the merit of the other group members' arguments, added his own question, "If Minerva is protecting us, then who is protecting her?"

"And who lurks in the shadows up there at the lake?" Atmun interjected with an ominous tone.

It soon became obvious that the group had probably solved one mystery only to be faced with another. They all sat in silence at the campfire near the base of the mountain and kept their thoughts and fears to themselves. Of course, they all knew the identity of the lurking shadows at Emerald Lake, but no one wished to discuss their suspicions openly.

At last, Deudal brought up the subject in specific terms. "We must assume that Minerva is in some desperate trouble. Why else would she act the way she did? I can't even imagine how painful it must have been for her to send us away. We must liberate her despite her attempt to save us! The Sutin emperor and his forces are responsible for Minerva's distress. I feel certain of it. However, we need a strategy. We must discover a way to reach Emerald Lake undetected and then find out if our companion is safe."

The Search for Minerva

While Dharmaji and the others discussed ways to summit Mount Dhala, Minerva remained captive by a platoon of Sutin infantry. The leader of the group, a muscular fiend, treated her cruelly and attempted to intimidate her, so she would reveal some secret he might find useful. Fortunately, however, the dim-witted officer had no notion of Minerva's true identity or capabilities.

Unknown to any of Sutin's soldiers, Minerva had employed her intuitive gift of bilocation. This movement through inner space had allowed her to warn her friends on the mountain in a way that Dharmaji and the others would secretly question. Minerva's harsh words and demeanor also served to frighten away anyone else who might be listening. Minerva had no idea, of course, that Sita had understood her message first.

Minerva also realized that if she simply sent out a signal for help, her friends might have all rushed up the mountain to save her regardless of the consequences. This would have proved disastrous. The Sutin's merciless warriors would have captured her friends; even Sita wouldn't have been spared. So, Minerva waited patiently and hoped her friends would have time to craft a viable plan.

To be sure, near the base of Mount Dhala, Dharmaji described a strategy that appeared to be amazingly simple, yet shrewd enough to offer the possibility of success. When he began to describe it, his faith in himself and his idea inspired the others.

"We've climbed this mountain once," he began slowly, "but a storm stopped us before we could reach the summit. However, tomorrow we will try again, but this time forming two independent teams. Atmun and I will ascend as we did yesterday. If a storm overtakes us, we'll return to the safest point that we reached on our last climb.

Meanwhile, Deudal and Sita will fly as high and as far up the mountain as possible. If the weather begins to freeze your wings, Deudal, you and Sita must land on the mountainside and build a fire intense enough to melt the ice from them. I've gathered a bundle of hardwood logs, and I'll give Sita a powerful flint stone.

If Atmun and I are fortunate enough to avoid any storms, we'll all meet near Emerald Lake. However, remember to stay away from the lake itself until we meet near the northern shore. Are there any questions?"

The Great Being's plan proved to be simple; yet, it required the others to reflect on it before they could respond. At last, Atmun asked probably the most obvious question. "Isn't this plan really dangerous, especially for Sita?"

Before Sita could answer, Dharmaji quickly replied. "Sita has been well prepared. She's intelligent and resourceful. Besides, it hardly seems fair to leave Minerva to her fate when she has just warned and protected us. Sita, what do you think?"

"I'm not afraid," the girl answered in a calm and reassuring tone. "Dharmaji is right. He's shown me many things, so now I must help. I won't leave your friend Minerva to die if I can do anything to prevent it. I won't leave her especially after she has risked her own safety not knowing if we could rescue her. She doesn't know me, yet she thought of my welfare over her own."

"Then it's settled," Dharmaji responded assertively. "We leave at dawn."

Meanwhile, high in the mountains at Emerald Lake, Minerva had already glimpsed Dharmaji's plan. Her intuition and logical reasoning had led her to the belief that her friends would soon attempt to deliver her from her Sutin captors. Nevertheless, she also realized that their attempt to free her had unforeseen difficulties which only she could truly comprehend. As she awaited their arrival, Minerva began to formulate her own strategy to assist them when they reached her. If she could only distract the unimaginative Sutin warriors long enough, she could assist them with her rescue.

While Minerva waited patiently for her comrades to arrive, the Mystic Being and his companions began their ascent toward Emerald Lake. Deudal positioned the firewood in Sita's pack and then hoisted her on his shoulders. Soon they both started climbing the mountainside hoping to avoid detection. At the same time, Atmun and Dharmaji began scrambling up the mountain trail as swiftly as their strength and the terrain would allow. By late afternoon, Sita and Deudal had approached the summit however; Dharmaji and Atmun were still only halfway to their objective of the lake.

Despite their success on the mountain, both Sita and Deudal recognized the need for caution and patience, so they built a crackling fire to keep them both from freezing. This also provided Dharmaji and Atmun with more time to reach them, so they could act in unison when it came time to liberate Minerva.

After sundown, Dharmaji and Atmun finally reached Sita and Deudal; then, without warning, another storm blew down from the mountain peak. Within a few hours, the fuel for the fire had burned to ash and the four would be liberators appeared in need of rescue themselves.

But their courage didn't fail them. Instead of retreating down the mountain a second time, they continued their journey with Deudal spreading his wings to partially block the impact of the howling wind and swirling snow. With Deudal in the lead, they reached the summit just as the Treeganaut's wings began to freeze. He fell to the ground and found it difficult to conceal his agony.

The team members knew they needed to act quickly. It became painfully clear to all that if Deudal didn't warm up soon, he would die. With the Sutin camp close by, it seemed obvious that the enemy warriors would probably be loitering around a lifesaving bonfire; and the camp itself would be, at least partially sheltered from the unforgiving storm. In order for Deudal to survive, he needed that fire.

Atmun, sensed that his friend Deudal might be in mortal danger, so he instantly transformed himself into a Sutin soldier and advanced directly into the enemy encampment. When the soldiers caught sight of him, they brandished their swords and waited for Atmun to speak. "I have captured one of the Treeganaut beasts, and I need help dragging him into camp," he called out.

Dharmaji took only a moment to understand that Atmun now pretended that Deudal was his prisoner, so he could lead him to the bonfire and save his life. He motioned for Sita to follow him, and they both silently slipped behind a sharp bend in the mountain trail, watching the scene unfold from their secret vantage point.

Amazingly, Atmun's transformation into a Sutin soldier totally deceived the enemy warriors. One soldier raced up to Deudal and helped the disguised Atmun drag the birdman over to their blazing fire. Then as Deudal slowly regained his senses, Atmun carefully scanned the camp to discover all he could. He identified twelve soldiers which seemed to be more than they had predicted. In addition, there appeared no sign of Minerva who remained, of course, the only reason he and his companions had ascended the mountain. In an effort to learn more about Minerva's whereabouts, Atmun tried to engage the soldiers in a conversation. "I thought I'd be alone up here on my hunting quest. What brings all of you up here?"

The soldiers seemed surprised by Atmun's question, and instead of answering, they became more aggressive. "We're all on this mountain for the same reason. Why don't you know?"

Atmun could feel himself losing his advantage and tried to recover. "Well, one thing is certain. I'm here to drag this Treeganaut right into your laps!"

This cunning remark probably saved Atmun and protected the rescue mission. Not only did it seemingly prove his allegiance, but it also cleverly deflected the soldier's threatening attitude. Even more importantly, Atmun's bravado also enticed one of the other soldiers to boast about Minerva. "You might have seized a birdman; but we've taken prisoner Minerva, the witch. That was the very purpose Emperor Sutin stationed us here in the first place. You just got lucky."

Despite the soldier's claim, Atmun still couldn't locate Minerva anywhere in the camp, so he decided to press the soldiers for a more detailed response. "You couldn't have captured that mystic hag! She's too clever for all of you!"

Right on cue, the officer in charge shouted haughtily, "Look behind that rock and you can see for yourself."

Atmun casually strolled behind the specific boulder that the soldier had pointed out, but it revealed nothing more than rock formations. Then he stared down on the ground and observed a huge chasm that looked at least twenty feet deep. There at the bottom; chained, gagged, and blindfolded lay Minerva seemingly unconscious or dead.

It became nearly impossible for Atmun to conceal the sorrow and anger that overwhelmed his heart. In an almost uncontrollable moment of rage, he felt tempted to attack all twelve soldiers on his own. But he quickly realized that his anger might very easily get his companions killed. So instead, he asked the soldiers more about their captive.

"I can't believe you captured her," Atmun began, attempting to sound surprised impressed.

"Yes," the Sutin leader proudly asserted. "The arrest of the old hag will greatly please the emperor. He's long suspected that she threatens his kingdom. Mostly, she frightens him because of her ability to cast treasonous spells. Now that we have both apprehended her and the Treeganaut, we'll be rewarded for bringing them to the emperor's city of Graganite. Now, retrieve the birdman and toss him into the pit. We'll break camp at first light tomorrow."

"Excuse me," Atmun spoke out, still disguised. "Shouldn't we finish thawing out the Treeganaut before we dump him in the cavern? Sutin himself may want to interrogate him before he severs his talons."

"Of course," the Sutin officer replied defensively. "That's what I meant. Finish thawing him out, and then dump him."

Dharmaji and Sita understood the crisis could worsen at any moment. The Mystic Being also knew that Atmun could not deceive the soldiers for long. He remained so concerned about Minerva and Deudal that he might impulsively defend them. Atmun might eventually attempt to confront the soldiers by again altering his appearance. This could further endanger the three companions and might even lead to their deaths.

Before long, the time for meaningful action arrived. Dharmaji, in a moment of spontaneity brought on by his concern, revealed his location by stepping directly into the enemy camp. He left Sita unprepared and frightened, as she waited behind in her hiding place. "Hello," Dharmaji said cordially to the first soldier he encountered. "I wish to speak to the officer in charge."

The soldier didn't respond to the Great Being's friendly tone. "I'm in charge!" he bellowed. "Who are you?"

"I, sir, am Emperor Sutin's health minister," Dharmaji yelled back. "I have been sent to quarantine all soldiers on this mountain who have been exposed to the plague."

The haughty officer now became less belligerent and condescending. "Are you suggesting the plague has broken loose again, Mr. Health Minister?"

"Yes, I am." Dharmaji answered. "The emperor is concerned the contagion will spread throughout his kingdom. I must examine all of you for fever, dizziness, and nodules."

"My soldiers haven't been infected," the officer insisted. "I would have certainly discovered the illness myself."

"You are not a physician!" Now I have travelled a great distance to do the emperor's will." Dharmaji responded forcefully, realizing that his ruse seemed to be working. "Shall I tell Emperor Sutin that you seem more qualified at diagnosing the plague than his chief health minister?"

The very suggestion that Sutin might be displeased clearly frightened the conceited officer, and he quickly amended his remarks. "I meant no disrespect. I just think I would have known if any of my soldiers looked ill. But go ahead and examine them."

"*Your* soldiers? Don't you mean the Emperor Sutin's soldiers?" Dharmaji pointedly asked.

"Yes, of course. The emperor's soldiers," the officer quickly replied.

With no further argument, the Sutin leader ordered his men to be examined by the kingdom's would be physician. Atmun, who had been tending to Deudal, hid quietly waiting for the Great One to reveal his real intentions. At last, after all twelve soldiers had been scrutinized; Dharmaji declared that the camp appeared to be free of disease. Dharmaji then called out to Sita. "Come, my child. The camp is safe."

Almost instantly, Sita wandered into the warriors' camp like a phantom. She quickly found her Mystic Teacher and said, "Thank goodness, Grandfather. "I was worried."

Before the Sutin leader could complain, the Great Being cut him off. "This is my granddaughter, Sita. She serves as the emperor's youngest food taster. Emperor Sutin wishes her to gather fruits and vegetables from every camp to determine if they're safe for him to eat.

Now feed her. She has no ill will toward any of you. She only wishes to help the emperor."

The Sutin soldiers did as ordered, but they certainly couldn't have anticipated what happened next. From behind the camp, Atmun left his secret lookout and stood before the soldiers at the campfire. He appeared very ill and exhibited all the symptoms of the deadly Crimson Plague. His body shook, he sweated profusely, and his chin and arms had dark boil-like nodules.

Dharmaji, still playing the role of chief health minister, acted outraged. "Why did you hide this soldier from me? This is treason!"

The officer acted so confused he could hardly speak. "He just wandered into camp at dawn!" he cried. "He hasn't even been around us!"

Atmun, understanding that his companion's entire intuitive plan seemed to be working, immediately fell down in the snow and pretended to lose consciousness.

The terror stricken soldiers felt too frightened to respond, so Dharmaji ordered, "Throw that soldier down into the cave with Minerva!"

The officer in charge immediately picked up on Dharmaji's mistake. "How did you know about the old witch?" he demanded, regaining a measure of control. Then he thought for a moment and yelled angrily, "It occurs to me that there are a number of coincidences happening all of a sudden. First, the solitary soldier surprises us with a Treeganaut, then a physician and his granddaughter suddenly appear trying to convince us there is a plague on the mountain. Worst of all, you all claim to be emissaries of Sutin himself, and yet you haven't shown us any real proof."

As soon as his harangue ended the officer ordered his soldiers to bind all four spies. Then he ordered the criminals to be guarded by the fire while he thought about what to do. He desperately needed to discover the truth about their identities and their purpose for infiltrating his camp. Clearly, they'd been lying about their identities; however, they still could be secret agents of the emperor. At last, his patience left him, and the officer decided to rely on his own brutality to interrogate them. He turned to one of his soldiers and ordered, "Throw the girl in the pit. If we don't hear the truth about this plot by dawn, we'll poison the 'food taster' with hemlock."

Dharmaji allowed the soldiers to toss Sita down into the cave, partly because he knew she might be strong enough to face her own fears, but mostly because she could assist Minerva. When the Mystic Teacher realized that his student appeared to be relatively safe, for a while, he told the officer the truth about their mission. He mentioned Minerva and how they needed to forge an alliance to confront the emperor in a way that would persuade him to improve the lives of the inhabitants of his kingdom. By the time he finished, Dharmaji already understood the consequences.

"You're traitors!" the officer bellowed furiously. "You'll be executed for your treachery, of that you can be certain!"

The brutal remarks of the Sutin leader sounded savage but understandable. It seemed obvious to the Great Being and all the other captives that they'd overestimated their own abilities and intelligence. If they couldn't defeat even twelve soldiers, how could they expect to overcome an entire army? It became clear that even stealth had failed them. The mission seemed over before it had truly begun.

Yet, sometimes what seems real is actually an illusion. While Sita attempted to assist Minerva by removing her shackles, she quickly discovered that Minerva's body felt virtually weightless. Indeed, it seemed to almost rise up and float likes a bubble through the air. Sita felt naturally frightened and confused by Minerva's condition, but she also considered the situation to be a possible sign of hope

Thankfully, Sita was correct in her assumption. Minerva who seemed frail and helpless had actually been waiting patiently for her friends to act. Now, certain that her comrades had done all they could on their own, she suddenly flew out of the cave and shot up high over the abyss. Then she hovered above the enemy camp, and created a terrifying spectacle of war such as cannon explosions, rifle volleys, and the horrifying cries of terrified soldiers. While the Sutin soldiers attempted to remain calm, Minerva's "attack" intensified, and within a quarter of an hour, the soldiers had scurried down the mountain like frightened children.

Dharmaji and the others all felt badly shaken until they apprehended that Minerva's powerful magic created all the chaos. When the enchantress seemed satisfied that the twelve soldiers wouldn't return, she untied the group and collected Sita from the frigid cavern. They reassembled by the fire and Atmun transformed back into his more sage like persona. He then asked Minerva the question that everyone else wanted to ask. "Minerva," he began respectfully, "why didn't you help us sooner? You knew we might be in trouble."

"I needed to know what you could accomplish on your own," Minerva replied simply. "Besides, I did help you by warning you."

"But Minerva," Deudal complained, "We only ascended to the lake in order to save you. Otherwise, we wouldn't have put ourselves in danger."

Now it was Minerva's turn to scold. "Do you think that Emperor Sutin has twelve conceited soldiers guarding his fortress at Graganite? If you're so easily defeated by twelve fighters, you'll certainly fail when challenged by more. You needed to find this out for yourself through your own experience."

This clear assessment embarrassed them all, of course, not because the statement seemed cruel, but because it was accurate. Dharmaji, who actually made the biggest blunder by announcing his knowledge of Minerva's presence, seemed perhaps the most to blame. He said nothing and waited for Minerva to continue. When she did, the entire group now felt unexpectedly inspired.

"Listen to me," she said mysteriously. "It's impossible for us to defeat the armies of Sutin. That isn't why we're together on this journey. Everything we think, say, and do can be possible sources of hope that may lighten the burdens of the citizens of Sutin's world. We must learn to walk forward by constantly falling down. Too much overconfidence, too early, brings out only selfishness and pride. But there is more. Tell them, Dharmaji."

The Mystic Being sat silently for a long time, and then he began to explain a mystery so deep that it appeared to be too difficult for the others to believe or even understand.

"Some of you here understand more about me than you've revealed, but now the time has come for all of you to know. I am Dharmaji, I'm also called Time Bender. My home world exists as a distant kingdom beyond the sky called Haventry. I have been here on your world for a thousand years seeking out individuals who may be worthy to join my fellow citizens on our world. My mission is defined by my power – Time Bending.

My purpose rests in my ability to help mortals overcome the thoughts and feelings that burden them with sorrow. By sojourning through time and creating an infinite number of difficult challenges, I make it possible for pilgrims to overcome their negative thoughts and beliefs. Then eventually, they may be able to live in harmony with themselves and the world around them. Over time, I can even teach some sojourners to transcend thought all together; first for minutes, then for days, and then, for even longer intervals. After sufficient experiences, when all thoughts have been mended and then overcome, it may be possible for mortals to inhabit my world."

Dharmaji's frightening and bizarre account seemed difficult for the group to totally apprehend. In addition, they couldn't grasp how Dharmaji's remarks could be hopeful to them personally. It seemed nearly impossible for them to understand that life itself could appear to be a kind of time driven drama created by Time Bender, simply to dredge up the groups' weaknesses and failings.

But Minerva didn't act surprised by Dharmaji's deep-thinking remarks. Her own testimony sounded equally shocking. "I too am originally from Haventry. Time Bender and I have been stationed here on Durgana for a very long time. We've been patiently searching for individuals of all races who seek to understand the significance of the 'One behind the many', those individuals who can glimpse a more evolved way of life."

"This compassionate attitude and intuitive ability are greatly needed at this time in your world," Minerva continued. "This planet of almost infinite capacity is slipping into darkness. Dharmaji, and possibly all of you, must turn back the darkness, so the light may once again shine through the gathering gloom and despair. Then, the light will illuminate your world again, and all beings who call this Durgana planet their home will again know peace and joy. But the time is short, and the light bearers remain few. We must move quickly and decisively."

Minerva's added explanation brought little comfort to the others. Her words induced more fear than hope within their heart and minds. Nevertheless, they now felt more certain that Minerva and Dharmaji could be telling the truth, no matter how confusing it sounded. As they sat quietly around the fire, the various group members began to think more deeply about the meaning of both Dharmaji and Minerva's enigmatic revelations. Before long, they all had questions about their own individual relationships with the two mystic beings.

Understandably, Atmun spoke first because he desperately wanted information about his true identity. His questions, directed at Dharmaji, sounded both simple and soulful. He gazed at Dharmaji with a piercing stare and asked, "Is it possible you and Minerva both know my true identity?"

"Yes, it's true," Time Bender replied simply. "I've always known who you are."

"And you never told me?" Atmun asked with a trace of anger rising in his voice.

"You wouldn't have understood," Dharmaji replied. "You cannot be told. You must learn the truth yourself."

"No more deceit!" Atmun shouted, finally becoming exasperated, "and no more clever words to avoid answering my questions. I want to know who I am, and I want to know now!"

"Very well," Minerva intervened. "I'll tell you the truth. You are nobody."

Atmun felt puzzled and irritated by the mystic's strange response. "How can I be nobody?"

Now, Dharmaji interrupted. "Atmun; Minerva has just given you the best answer that you can understand at the moment. Clearly, you can transform into any mortal, and yet none of these transformations can be who you truly are. So, while you sojourn with us, you are 'nobody', at least for now."

These unintelligible replies to Atmun's desperate inquires became too much for the old man to bear, and he began to weep. As he sank into the depths of despair, Sita approached him with a measure of comfort far beyond the capacity of most young people. "Atmun, we're all really nobody when you think about it. We don't know where we've come from, and in many ways, we don't understand where we are right now. It's all part of an illusion, a dream in which we're all somehow asleep. I believe the answers to all our questions lie before us on our journey even if we don't know where we will finish."

"The answer also remains within you, Atmun," Dharmaji softly added. "You must solve this riddle on your own. In fact, it would probably be helpful if we all considered ourselves to be 'nobody' because that can be a kind of subtle identity for us. Now enough word play, the time has come for action. The fortress city of Graganite exists only a few miles away beyond the next Mountain pass. We need to advance in that direction and devise a plan along the way. It's time to forget our own wants and needs for the good of the Durgana world."

The other team members, realizing their questions would now go unanswered, kept their doubts and suspicions to themselves. Their own personal histories would have to wait for a more auspicious time.

The Conflict of Good and Evil Commences

With Dharmaji as commander and Minerva as counselor, the small band of revolutionaries traversed the mountain pass stopping only long enough to uncover the narrow trail. Because of Minerva's mystical tracking ability, she soon discovered short cuts and switch backs running along the steep and dangerous slopes. This allowed the group to save precious energy and time. Unfortunately, however, despite their impending confrontation, no one could formulate a proposal for their attack, or if they could, they weren't sharing it with the others.

Despite this inability to devise a plan; the group traveled close enough to the fortress at Graganite to at least observe its defenses and the dilapidated village huddled beside it. As they carefully studied the scene from their hiding place on the mountain, they could see a huge castle rising through the sky. They could also discern enemy soldiers stationed at every turret with even more sentries stationed at the base of the fortress itself. Around the entire structure was a foul looking moat that stretched out one hundred yards in all directions. Beyond the moat, the poverty stricken villagers could be observed laboring in the fields and tending their livestock. From their vantage point Dharmaji and the others could also see Sutin soldiers terrorizing the farmers with wild gestures and strident commands. Before long, the band of rebels on the ridge realized their task looked impossible.

Alone and uncertain, Minerva and the others huddled together throughout the night near the castle. They conversed all night attempting to create a strategy that might prove helpful and effective. Just before dawn, Dharmaji, yet again, pointed out the purpose of their mission. "Remember," he advised. "We don't need to defeat Sutin and his forces. We simply need to find a way to allow the light to expand."

"Then we must defeat Emperor Sutin, at least!" Deudal suddenly asserted forcefully. "He's responsible for the kidnapping of the entire Treeganaut race! He must die!"

"No," Minerva sharply replied. "We won't defeat evil with evil. Not here. Not now. You see the vast army that Sutin commands. We can't challenge them all directly. We need something much more subtle. What we need is an illusion; a deception so powerful that everyone in the fortress and the village will become terror stricken."

"Yes," replied Dharmaji. "We need to create an alternate portrayal of their Graganite world. We need a trick of the light."

"What do you mean exactly?" Atmun asked with interest.

"Almost everyone accepts reality as it is presented to him," Dharmaji continued. "What's the one thing that almost all beings are afraid to ponder?"

"Death," Deudal broke in. "Death is the one thing that terrifies almost all beings."

"Correct," Dharmaji agreed. "So, we must create the illusion that death is arriving. Now, how can we do that?"

The group members remained silent for an excruciatingly long time, but at last Sita came up with the perfect solution which they all so desperately needed. "We could create the illusion that the world is ending. We could make everyone believe that the world will soon be destroyed."

"Yes," Minerva answered for everyone. "Sita's idea offers the deceptions of fear, instability, and surprise. If Sutin and his armies believe the world may be ending, they could break ranks and scatter in confusion. Even Sutin himself will be terrified if he believes he can't live for eternity, especially if there appears to be no location for his eternity to exist!"

The five group members now all truly felt excited about Sita's idea, because they all recognized an opportunity to employ their own unique strengths and experiences against Sutin and his troops.

With a glimmer of hope now finally providing a sense of direction and purpose, the group of interlopers began discussing their plans in more specific detail. Minerva, perhaps the most gifted of all the team members, began the discussion as if she might be casting roles in a play. "Atmun, you'll be our fearless prophet who will convince the inhabitants of Graganite that the judgment day has arrived. Deudal, you'll become the merciless dragon who punishes the wicked; and Sita you'll be cast as the orphan who persuades the citizenry that the prophet speaks the truth."

"While Minerva and I," Dharmaji added enthusiastically, "will create phantoms, illusions, and feelings of dread that'll take root within the minds of Sutin and his entire kingdom."

When Minerva and the Dharmaji finished, an undeniable feeling of awkwardness spread among the group members. Despite Dharmaji and Minerva's overpowering self-confidence, the others weren't so easily convinced. Remembering their many failures in the past, they felt uneasy about a scheme so quickly conceived and alarmingly short on details. Even worse, when Sita and Deudal turned to discuss their concerns with Minerva and Dharmaji, the two powerful outworlders had vanished.

The three remaining team members now felt disappointed and more than a little frightened, but they knew that Minerva and Dharmaji could sometimes suddenly disappear. Their disappearances challenged the ingenuity and perseverance of the other group members and also tested their courage. These trials usually focused on emotional growth and spiritual maturity. Nonetheless, these present circumstances felt different both in intensity and importance. The drama that would soon be acted out had a compelling sense of significance about it. This simple truth led all three group members to doubt themselves and question the judgment of the two powerful friends.

"This plan seems like an impossible situation," Deudal complained. "How are we going to perform these tasks with no direction or assistance?"

"You're right," Atmun concurred. "We've no strategy to attack Sutin or his forces. It must mean that Minerva and Dharmaji want us to remain here until they return."

"No," Sita answered flatly. "This plan must include all of us even now. We all know that Dharmaji has disappeared before, and sometimes at crucial moments. In the past, I felt certainly angered and confused by this lack of direction, but it's important for us to begin the deception now without waiting for more details."

Deudal and Atmun still remained cautious, but they dared not reveal their trepidation especially in front of such an extraordinary child. So without further debate, they approached the village.

When the three actors approached their destination, they gathered their courage and hiked through the woods that bordered the shabby Graganite village. When they reached the shacks nearest their position, they halted in order to plan their next move. However, just when their conversation began in earnest; Atmun unexpectedly raced into the village street, and began shouting obscure prophesies about the end of the world.

Meanwhile, Minerva, sensing Atmun's movements, created her first illusion by using her magic power. Incredibly, she blocked out the sun behind dark and ominous clouds. Atmun, aware and deeply appreciative of Minerva's intervention, yelled out even louder shouting:

"Citizens of Graganite! Hear me well! The Day of Judgment approaches! The time to change your ways has come! Your world is doomed! The end has come at last! You must turn from your wickedness while there's still time!"

Unfortunately, but also predictably, this spectacle directed by Minerva wasn't frightening enough to actually intimidate the arrogant soldiers. Instead, it created a sense of terror in only the villagers who immediately scooped up their children and fled into their hovels. Before long, only the Sutin warriors remained out on the street and they looked angry. They deeply resented Atmun's sudden power over the town and they quickly surrounded the solitary figure. Seizing him by the neck, they demanded, "Who are you?"

Atmun whether in fear or inspiration uttered the first words that entered his mind. "I am nobody."

The soldiers interpreted Atmun's statement as deceitful and insolent, so they threw him to the ground and bound his hands behind his back. When it became clear that Atmun wasn't going to be rescued, he cried out, "Minerva, Dharmaji, help me!"

When no response occurred, the soldiers grabbed Atmun by the arms, dragged him to his feet, and then led the bewildered soothsayer toward the castle and Sutin's court.

Horrified, Sita and Deudal retreated into the shadows of the forest. Now it was their turn to enter the scene. Deudal, remembering his role as dragon, covered his body and wings with bright vermilion ochre from a nearby stream bed. Sita following Deudal's example, covered her arms, face, and clothes with mud and leaves. When they felt ready, the two actors entered the village and approached the remaining soldiers.

Meanwhile, Minerva continued her horrific spell by adding lightning, thunder, and a driving rain to her spectacle. Sita, in a moment of courage shouted, "You've seized the prophet, but you can't ignore his warning! The Day of Judgment is here! Surrender your weapons and repent! This ferocious dragon, you see beside me, is from the underworld, and soon he will strike, destroying the arrogant warriors of Sutin!"

At first, the soldiers seemed captivated by Sita's bravery and sincerity, but as the downpour persisted, Deudal's vermillion disguise and Sita's mud began to wash off. Soon the soldiers grew more brazen and sarcastic as they closely observed Deudal and Sita's simple disguises. The soldier's began to retaliate. One stout soldier mocked, "You're a meddlesome little witch and your horrifying dragon is just a disgraced Treeganaut who must have been cowering in the woods until now!"

"It seems that you Treeganauts are always hiding!" Another soldier jeered mockingly. "Did the girl help you with your 'terrifying' dragon costume?"

Before long, the lead officer spoke up. "Take the birdman to the castle and let him join his friends!"

"What about the child?" another soldier inquired.

"Let her go," the officer ordered. "Maybe if we release her, she'll bring another birdman to us!"

The soldiers all enjoyed their superior's sarcastic barbs, and they followed his order. After restraining Deudal, the troops departed from the village with the birdman following them tethered to a coarse rope. Deudal felt defeated and alone, and his only comfort was that he remained by Sita's side even though he could have easily glided away. The Sutin officer freeing Sita also gave Deudal the sense that he felt partially responsible for her escape.

Meanwhile, Atmun, surrounded by soldiers, had crossed the bridge over the putrid moat and had entered the Sutin's intimidating fortress. He felt alone not only due of his own failure, but also because Dharmaji and Minerva seemed unwilling to rescue him. As the soldiers thrust him through the gate and bullied him down the stairs to his rat infested cell, he seemed so melancholy that even death appeared to be a better fate.

Yet, despite Atmun's genuine feelings of terror and gloom, he discovered that others might be imprisoned with him. After the soldiers left, he finally regained control of his unreliable emotions and recognized the Great Being in the adjacent dungeon cell. In a shriek of excitement, he yelled, "Dharmaji. Is that really you?"

"Lower your voice!" the mystic prisoner whispered harshly. "If the guards find out we're friends, they're sure to separate us."

Atmun instantly lowered his voice and asked, "How did you get here?"

Dharmaji laughed softly and replied, "I just strolled in through the front door, so to speak. But how did you get here, Atmun? I thought you agreed to proclaim judgment day by assuming the role of a prophet."

"I did," Atmun replied becoming dejected again. "But the soldiers arrested me after only a few minutes. So, I have been no help at all."

"Don't be so sure," the Great Teacher reassured. "It became necessary for both of us to be captured. Your prophetic words acted as prompts that were needed, so the soldiers would take you before Sutin."

"I don't understand," Atmun replied in confusion. "How does getting captured further our plan?"

Dharmaji smiled and answered, "Sutin will soon have a very bad nightmare, and you will be his tormenter."

"Do you really mean I'm supposed to be locked up in this filthy cell?" Atmun asked incredulously.

Yes," Dharmaji replied. "But now we must get you prepared for your audience with Sutin and his court. He will have his prophetic dream tonight, and you will be brought before him tomorrow. Sutin doesn't realize you're imprisoned here yet, but tomorrow the guards will escort you to his throne, and you'll be tried for treason."

Dharmaji's statement terrified his friend. "How will I defend myself when I appear before Sutin? What should I say?"

"What did you say to the soldiers in the village?" Dharmaji inquired.

"I told them that I am nobody," Atmun answered feebly.

"Good. Very good," Dharmaji exclaimed. "I want you to continue repeating that exact statement tonight and tomorrow. Do you understand what it means yet?"

"I am nobody suggests that every disguise I assume will eventually fade away, so one specific identity can never be permanent. In addition, the absence of these identities reveals the silent background from which my disguises appear. So, in essence 'nobody' is the background behind 'everybody' and 'everything.'"

"Yes, yes," the Great Mystic concurred excitedly. "It's like gathering a ball of yarn that is made up of your thoughts. Thoughts that you've created like gathering different colored strands. When all the strands are removed, nothing is left. Likewise, even thoughts, or in your case, every transformation, is only an illusion you might believe to be real."

"And we accept reality as it's presented to us," Atmun emphatically replied, remembering Dharmaji's earlier words. "But how do we use this knowledge to our advantage?"

"We must create an illusion for Sutin and his court to witness," Dharmaji answered mysteriously. "It's important that you don't change form, no matter what happens, and you must continue to identify yourself in the same manner as you've been doing with the soldiers."

"Do you mean I should continue to say that 'I am nobody'?" Atmun asked pointedly.

"Yes," Dharmaji solemnly replied. "But you must also do something else. I want you to observe everything from now on without trying to interpret it."

"I'm lost," Atmun said with a look of uncertainty. "What do you mean?"

"It means you must see everything as it exists without adding or subtracting your own thoughts and impressions. In other words keep your mind open."

"I still don't understand," Atmun answered, more confused than ever.

"Look at these iron bars and tell me what you see," Dharmaji instructed.

"I see iron bars that still keep us prisoners. The bars can't be bent by me and I will probably never see the outside world of Durgana again," Atmun sighed, drifting back into despair.

The Great Being smiled knowingly and replied, "All you really see are the iron bars. Everything else describes your own thoughts, fears, and imagination."

Atmun remained skeptical, "But how will keeping an open mind help us?

"Soon, Minerva and I will begin to create more strange illusions and dreams that are meant to affect King Sutin and the citizenry of Graganite," Dharmaji whispered. "You must realize that these deceptions remain unreal, so you don't panic. Then you won't do anything impulsive like Sutin's court and the inhabitants. Now, practice the awareness of nothingness. You'll need this skill by tomorrow. Also, try to rest."

Atmun followed his friend's instructions, but he felt uncertain and vulnerable about the great teacher's guidance. No matter how he focused his mind, it still seemed anxious causing him to question his courage.

Meanwhile, the plight of Deudal looked much more troubling than the immediate circumstances of either, Atmun or Dharmaji. The birdman had become a valuable trophy for the Emperor Sutin. Deudal was paraded through the castle like a sacred relic. By the time he reached the foul smelling dungeon, he had already seen his Treeganaut comrades either stuffed as wall sculptures, or dismembered for jewelry.

The awful brutality of it all left Deudal outraged and nauseous. When he ultimately ended up in his cell, he felt consumed by rage and despair. However, Atmun and Dharmaji remained exceedingly careful not to reveal themselves until the guards disappeared behind a stone wall.

After the guards had disappeared, Atmun spoke first. "Deudal. Dharmaji and I are here. Don't be afraid."

"I'm not afraid!" Deudal shot back. "I'm angry!"

Dharmaji again cautioned both his friends to lower their voices and then remarked, "It's almost dawn. The time for our deliverance is nearly here. Soon the guards will come to escort us to Sutin. Be ready."

Meanwhile, as Dharmaji continued counseling his fellow prisoners, Sita appeared to be abandoned, wandering alone in the forest. She couldn't comprehend all that had occurred, but she remained determined to persevere, if she only knew what to do. After several hours of aimlessly searching for any useful trail or clue, she suddenly happened upon Minerva, the great conjurer herself.

"Don't be afraid, child," Minerva declared. "You and I will do our part to save the villagers and rescue our friends."

Sita certainly seemed excited to see Minerva, but she felt less convinced about the mystic's optimism. "We've been easily defeated every time we've faced the enemy," Sita pointed out. "In fact, you can't even call them defeats. We've simply surrendered without a fight and allowed the Sutin soldiers to arrest us. What kind of plan is that?"

"A good plan," Minerva replied, ignoring Sita's tone. "Now the trap is set."

Naturally Sita saw their circumstances very differently. "Yeah; but we're the ones who appear to be trapped!"

Before Sita could continue expressing her doubts, Minerva had already begun striding down the cobblestone road directly toward the Graganite Castle. Fearing she would be left behind again, Sita ran to catch up. As they trekked down the royal road and approached the castle moat, not a single soldier attempted to detain them. At first, Sita assumed that the soldiers didn't consider them to be a threat, so they ignored them. However, when Minerva jumped on to the drawbridge, Sita realized they were invisible and free to advance at will.

As Minerva and Sita freely moved through the opulent palace chambers and crossed the cold ivory halls, they finally discovered the emperor's throne room. When they entered, Minerva paused and waited patiently for the evil despot to appear. Sita, completely mystified by Minerva's movements, remained courageous and silent despite her anxiety. She dared not even imagine what her powerful friend intended doing, but she also felt very afraid to leave her side.

Sita could never have predicted the events that unfolded before her as the dawn illuminated the castle. Sutin had anxiously entered the chamber with all his petty advisors walking humbly behind him. As he traversed the room, it became very clear that something appeared to be terribly wrong. Sutin's appearance looked wildly disheveled and his voice so high pitched he sounded like a whining child. Frantically darting around the room, Sutin acted as if something could be pursuing him. When he finally sat down, an advisor with a long beard, sunken eyes, and a gnarled body approached the king. "What did you see, my emperor? Tell me your vision."

Sutin gazed piercingly at his advisor and then at the wall and exclaimed, "I had a dream that the end of the world has come. A ghost kept shouting, 'You are nobody! The day of doom is here. You are nobody!'"

The advisor shook his head repeatedly in mock solemnity and answered, "My emperor, you just experienced a bad dream. It must have been some phantom of your imagination. Perhaps you ate a tainted piece of meat. Do not worry yourself."

Sutin, in no mood for condescending explanations turned on his advisor and demanded, "Would you barter your life on that counsel?"

The advisor appeared stunned, but then replied more submissively, "I am certain, my Lord."

This affirmation might have helped pacify the emperor if the dungeon guards hadn't brought Atmun, Dharmaji, and Deudal into the center of the chamber. As soon as the prisoners appeared, the emperor became even more frightened. The guards, however, were unaware of the events that had just taken place before their arrival with their three prisoners.

After knocking Atmun to the floor, they demanded that he speak his name. "Tell the emperor your name!" one guard sneered gleefully.

"I am nobody," Atmun replied simply.

The guards, who expected the entire court to break out into peals of laughter, were horrified to discover that Sutin became enraged. He immediately ordered the arrest of the guards, and then he glared at Atmun.

Suddenly, in an uncontrollable frenzy, the delirious emperor abruptly lunged at Atmun and dashed his head against the ivory palace floor. This represented the moment for all Atmun's friends to rally to his side. They all attempted to separate Sutin from his half-conscious victim, but the remaining palace guards immediately prevailed against Dharmaji and the others.

Before long, a violent and chaotic scene began to unfold. Minerva, who, like Sita, remained undetectable, created a hellish vision that terrified the entire court. In this demonic projection, towering flames and fiendish cries swept through the palace overwhelming everyone with feelings of horror and dread. Dharmaji, anticipating Minerva would act, liberated Atmun from the infuriated Sutin who began reeling around like a wounded beast. Deudal, seeking revenge, found an outlet for his intense rage and tackled the disoriented dungeon guards even though he actually believed Minerva's terrifying conjuring was real.

Soon, the entire castle descended into a state of turmoil. Servants deserted their stations, and soldiers shouted hysterically as they endeavored to lower the castle drawbridge. The magical inferno and piercing screams pervaded every chamber with horrifying intensity until Sutin himself felt both physically and mentally overcome.

Encouraged by her success, Minerva expanded her enchantment beyond the castle walls, out through the village, and into the countryside. This greatly amplified the spell's noxious effect, and the soldiers and even the villagers were engulfed by the same chaotic cloud that had inundated the castle. Soon the entire kingdom of Sutin appeared to be under siege, controlled by Minerva who seemed almost possessed by her own incantation. Her only connection outside her powerful illusion proved to be Sita standing beside her.

As Minerva's elaborate deception grew more intense, Sutin, fearing for his own safety, approached Atmun in utter despair. Sutin's countenance revealed that he had been nearly frightened to death. His advisors had fled from his side in terror. Sutin again asked Atmun to reveal his identity. "Who are you?" he cried out.

In the meantime, Dharmaji intervened before Atmun could respond. "He is nobody like all the rest of us."

The Great One's remark had a strangely calming effect on the tyrant. He stood suddenly quiet amid the chaotic vision, and his fear subsided. He removed the Treeganaut necklace from around his bruised neck, and Minerva slowly dissolved her terrifying spell. It became a transformative moment for Emperor Sutin.

In his time of terror and despair, he felt a sense of freedom beyond his kingdom and even his mortal frame. It suddenly occurred to him that immortality might already be the possible condition of all beings. The emperor's induced delusion, both in the nightmare and in Minerva's horrific drama, had pushed him out of his selfishness. Now he glimpsed out at a world of peace and silence that had been completely unknown to him.

Equally astonishing, Atmun also felt deeply affected by his own response to Minerva's spell casting. By following Dharmaji's instructions, Atmun discovered the secret of his identify at last. Even when Sutin wrestled him to the ground, Atmun still chanted 'I am nobody' and remained focused. Then the miraculous happened. As Atmun hit the ground, he surrendered his mind to the river of energy within himself. For one brief moment, he merged with the ocean of light and bliss. When he returned to his body a few moments later, Dharmaji lifted him up off the ground and called his name.

Nonetheless, it took quite some time before Minerva's fiendish spectacle dissipated, and by then Atmun already felt compassion for Sutin. The emperor's appearance now looked much more subdued and even repentant.

But Deudal remained far less understanding. As soon as circumstances allowed, he lunged at Sutin and probably would've killed him if the others hadn't intervened. "You are a fiend!" the birdman yelled. "Now all my people are dead. Dead, because of you!"

After Dharmaji and the soldiers finally rescued Sutin from Deudal's razor-sharp talons, Sutin made a stunning revelation. "Your Treeganaut friends aren't dead. Many remain imprisoned on one of my islands."

"That's a lie! What about the stuffed trophies and jewelry?" Deudal challenged.

"They weren't murdered," Sutin replied meekly. "I scavenged the trophies. Those bird beings had been dead before we even kidnapped any of the others. The truth is the talons don't grant immortality. If they did, I would have slept much better at night."

Deudal still felt agitated, but now he also seemed hopeful for the first time in years, demanded that the emperor reveal the exact location where his people remained captive. Without a moment's hesitation, Sutin answered, "I'll do better than that. I'll bring them to you, right here, right now."

The chastened emperor took a hollow reed from his back pocket and began whistling a high pitched tune that sounded so forceful; it became impossible to endure without everyone covering his ears. At the same time, Minerva and Sita walked out of their invisible space and approached the others.

A few minutes later, as Sutin put down his pipe and began describing his newly acquired understanding of life, the sky grew dark as midnight as singing chants filled the air. High in the clouds, the Treeganauts appeared.

Over a thousand birdlike beings descended on the castle, swooped down to the turrets, and glided to the ground. Then, the creatures carefully searched every area of the castle grounds seeking Deudal, the last relative who had been left behind. Somehow they knew that his courage and perseverance must have been at least partly responsible for their liberation. When he finally appeared to his comrades, Deudal seemed to recognize every single individual of his nation. Before long the entire castle resembled a gigantic aviary.

However, once the reunion occurred, there still remained the dangerous problem of Sutin and his warriors. It didn't seem prudent to allow Sutin to remain in power, especially since he had been the architect of such a monstrous realm. Even his promise to reform himself seemed too hasty a conversion for one whose entire life relied on deceit and conquest.

Most importantly, Deudal didn't believe Sutin's conversion could be plausible. The very idea that a wicked tyrant could forever change his actions wasn't something that Deudal intended to believe. The emperor's treachery and deceit remained notorious in the Graganite kingdom. Deudal remained deeply suspicious of Sutin's seemingly genuine change of heart. Even as he gazed at the Treeganaut multitude together at last; Deudal understood that Sutin could have easily massacred them at any time. When they had been island prisoners in his dungeons, he might well have acted impulsively and tortured them as well.

Whether it happened to protect his people or because he sought revenge, Deudal finally decided to act and end the threat to his race permanently. As everyone seemed to be on the verge of celebrating, the giant birdman suddenly rushed over to Sutin and pulled him into the sky. Gripping him with his talons, Deudal ascended mercilessly, while the emperor shrieked out in fear, pleading for his life. Deudal flew high above the clouds and then, suddenly released him, and the emperor cruelly plummeted to his death. Everyone present felt sickened by Deudal's unforeseen wickedness and brutality.

Everyone except the Treeganauts. They began crying out in triumph at the tyrant's demise. Their incarceration on the islands with no trees or sky had made them miserable for countless years. When they witnessed Sutin's death, they felt overwhelming joy and gratitude. They all rushed to Deudal and raised him on their shoulders as the conquering hero. Finally, as the initial excitement abated, Deudal approached Dharmaji and the others saying, "I don't know if you agree with what I've just done, but eliminating Sutin has offered my people freedom and peace. Our world has been redeemed, now that the tyrant is dead."

"Yes!" Dharmaji suddenly burst out. "You replaced one tyrant with a new one! Your first official act as a leader, Deudal, has been to execute your enemy!"

"But Dharmaji," Deudal replied defensively. "Now my people will be safe. From now on we will rule Durgana with compassion."

Dharmaji had seen and heard enough. As he and the others turned to leave, he made one last poignant remark. "Just remember, Deudal. You've committed murder, and you now believe your Treeganaut race should be considered the most important. So, how do you think you've the necessary qualities of humility and compassion to be a truly just ruler for all?"

Deudal felt hurt by Dharmaji's caustic remarks, but he also realized that no amount of persuasion would alter the Great Mystic's judgment. Although he didn't regret his decision to kill Sutin, he did feel disappointed that he'd never see his truly great, compassionate friend again. Nevertheless, Deudal's Treeganaut race clearly did understand his motives and their love and support would help him to overcome his loss.

With nothing more to say, Dharmaji, Minerva, Atmun, and Sita headed toward the drawbridge in silence. The climax to their mission remained far from satisfactory because one evil emperor had simply been replaced by another possible tyrant. Perhaps Deudal would be a wiser and more compassionate leader than Sutin; but Deudal had the character traits of anger and revenge. These failings could blossom into hatred over time, and the future of the Graganite Kingdom appeared to be in doubt yet again. Perhaps life would get better, but the kingdom itself would certainly not become a utopian paradise.

The final scene of the Great One's drama was yet to unfold. As they all stepped across the gap between the drawbridge and the far side of the moat, Sita fell through the open space and bumped her head losing external consciousness.

When Sita woke up, she found herself sitting in a beautiful rock cavern high in the recesses of the Dhala Mountains. All around her a tangible stillness seemed interrupted only by a small crackling fire beside her. She experienced a secret tranquility and felt deeply inspired by her new surroundings. As she acclimated herself to the gentle sounds from the fire, she enjoyed a joyful sense of freedom. In her silent stillness, Sita could even hear her own breath and feel the rhythm of her slow beating heart. She held the vision diligently until the Great Being appeared to her.

"You've done well," Dharmaji whispered. "You've found that the mind creates the worlds. At last, you've arrived here, beyond the worlds of selfishness."

"Where is here?" Sita asked respectfully.

"This realm is the clarity of your own mind," her Mystic Teacher answered. "All the stories and characters we create are just illusions and dreams, which exist in space and time as nobody and everybody."

"How can you say we create our experiences?" Sita asked.

"You must know my name, child," Dharmaji answered, shaping the conversation. "I am you. You separated yourself from me. All your trials, triumphs, and defeats are really the thoughts and feelings you've experienced so you could finally reach this mountain retreat."

"So none of my experiences have been real?" Sita asked in confusion.

"No, child. Only the light and love are real," the Great Being replied simply. "Everything else exists in the world of change. They are impermanent worlds through which we pass."

"Please, Dharmaji," Sita implored. "Explain it in an easier way."

"All right," her teacher asserted. "Individuals of the Durgana world are asleep, but they don't realize it. Some inhabitants, however, may be partially awake, and a few are wide awake. You discovered my image because you were partly awake, so there exists real hope for you."

"Are you saying that most people still live in the dark as if they were dreaming," Sita asked.

"Yes," Dharmaji conceded. "Now you have a choice. Do you wish to remain here in happiness and safety, or do you wish to help the dreamers awaken?"

Sita sat quietly for a long time pondering the implications of Dharmaji's difficult question. Finally, she replied, "Shouldn't we wish for everyone to wake up, even if it's painful for all of us at times?"

"Yes," Dharmaji warmly agreed. "And we must also remember that no one can harm our true selves."

As the setting sun dipped lower in the sky outside the mouth of the cave, twilight began to create shadows on the dimming wall. "I'm ready to travel again," Sita said softly. "I wish to help others who need to find their way."

"So be it," replied Dharmaji.

"When will we leave?" Sita asked with anticipation.

"Is now soon enough?" The Mystic Teacher replied.

SOJOURNERS THROUGH TIME

<The End>

93

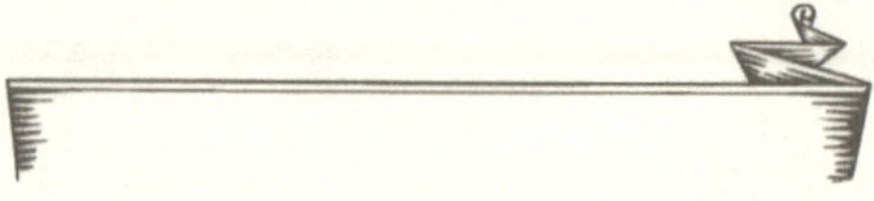

Books By John Frederick Zurn

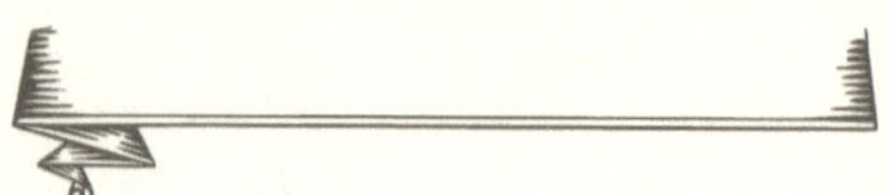

MENTAL HEALTH
The End Justifies the Pain
The Promise of Long Term Recovery
The Bipolar Challenge
Memoirs of a Bipolar Soul
Metamorphosis:
from Mental Illness to Spiritual Awakening

SPIRITUAL EXPERIENCES
This Moment Called God
Passing Through the Dream
One Hundred Devotional Poems
Poems of Hope and Inspiration
100 Simple Prayers

FICTION : Sojourners Through Time
Non-Fiction: The Comedy in Everyday Life

Don't miss out!

Visit the website below and you can sign up to receive emails whenever John Frederick Zurn publishes a new book. There's no charge and no obligation.

https://books2read.com/r/B-A-IHPT-GOJYB

BOOKS 2 READ

Connecting independent readers to independent writers.

Did you love *Sojourners Through Time*? Then you should read *The End Justifies the Pain : Writings About Mental Health*[1] by John Frederick Zurn!

[2]

John chronicles some of his bipolar episode experiences, both in-patient and outpatient;, and how he has achieved long term recovery. He details the process of identifying the appropriate medication and the importance of consistent usage. He identifies a variety of coping skills - how to develop and use them. John then delves into how creative expression can channel thoughts and emotions in useful and constructive ways, psychological and spiritual. As examples of John's creative process, he includes 2 of his short stories and 17 poems.

Read more at https://www.portalstoinnerdimensions.com/.

---

1. https://books2read.com/u/md68RW

2. https://books2read.com/u/md68RW

www.ingramcontent.com/pod-product-compliance
Lightning Source LLC
Chambersburg PA
CBHW051901130726
47987CB00002B/934